A
DEMAIN

Joe Tom King

ARCHWAY
PUBLISHING

Archway Publishing books may be ordered through booksellers or by contacting:

Archway Publishing
1663 Liberty Drive
Bloomington, IN 47403
www.archwaypublishing.com
844-669-3957

ISBN: 978-1-4808-9269-9 (sc)
ISBN: 978-1-4808-9268-2 (hc)
ISBN: 978-1-4808-9270-5 (e)

Library of Congress Control Number: 2020913203

Print information available on the last page.

Archway Publishing rev. date: 10/14/2020

Doubt thou the
stars are fire
Doubt that the
sun doth move
Doubt truth to
be a liar
But never
Doubt
I Love

Bill Shakespeare

A DEMAIN

I HAVE BEEN DEAD for six years now. Not really dead, just lonesome. There have been no relationships in my life; I don't even have a dog. I couldn't count Renfroe, my law partner, or Arlene, my legal assistant for the past fifteen years. I was a complete and utter pauper in the arena of love and affection. I have been married twice and am now zero for two in that endeavor, no kids from either one I wanted to have two kids, one would be named Leviticus and the other Acts. My marriages had conflagrations not conversations. I had nothing but new clothes to show for my marriages, the last wife started a major fire in our front yard and burned every piece of clothing I owned. Thereby, forcing me to rebuy, again, more stuff.

I was subsumed by tristesse, known by the French as sadness. So much that I went to the library every Saturday by myself and read the New York Times and the Wall Street Journal. Last Saturday, I was sitting across the table from a small female. She had on a camouflage pattern shirt but the colors were green and pink. Her eight teeth were a dull yellow, the same color as her fingernails. On top of her head was a ball cap that said "Wizards." Her shoes were Michael Jordan knock off- sneakers. I must have been staring at her. She looked at me with a serious frown on her face and said, "You know if you had any goddamn sense at all, you would get your ass up and leave here. Quit staring."

I took her advice and left the building. At least the weather was clean and neat. The air felt like feathers on my face. I felt like I was stumbling along; shambling is a better word to describe my movement. The hangover that I had earned the previous night was no help at all.

Walking directly at me was a tall lady. She strolled towards me like a sine wave. I could not help it; I just stopped. If she were a painting, people would pull up a chair and look at it for hours. It was like I had been hit with a truncheon, and the only thought mustered was, "je ne sais quoi." I did not know what it was, but I was struck. She was dressed like a runway model. Her clothes whispered of confidence, sophistication, and general well-being. I wanted to hide so she could not see me. I didn't have to worry about that, she did not waste a glance in my direction.

For days, she flowed through my mind like smooth silver. My brain had been commandeered.

The following Friday night I received a mercy invitation for dinner with a group from another law firm in town. I arrived late due to a conference with Renfroe, which required a couple of solid bourbon drinks to justify our verdict. I walked to the table and there she was. There is a god who still has my name on his list. Thank you Jesus. I sat cattycornered from her and just hunkered there like a country boob with a drink in his hand. One week in time had only burnished her beauty. She was involved in a conversation with another lady, who I did not know. The evening evaporated and the only thing I had to show for it was her name, Katie. Words between us were scarce and non-committal. There was no bolt of lightning. But I knew that I had entered her kiln.

And so, it began.

Hot Monkey Sex. Yes, that is what it was...Katie smiled at me, then kissed me on the mouth. We were both way past the hot monkey sex qualifying age but anytime we made love that lasted less than ten minutes, we declared it HMS... And then we would laugh like hell... God, we had fun and still do. We are probably the only couple that has a sex qualifier known as SOS. Socks on Sex, because when you are average age of sixty-seven and one half, sometimes it is too much trouble to get your socks off and even more trouble to get them back on.

After she kissed me, we laid on our backs, held hands, and talked. What are we listening to? We always listened to music. She loves Norah Jones and James Taylor; I like Lyle Lovett, St. Paul and the

Broken Bones, and Mike and the Moonpies. One of our favorite things is for one of us to discover someone in the music milieu that neither one of us had known before.

About two months ago, I read a story about Gary Stewart in the Oxford American Magazine. It was like finding a rara avis at a neighborhood yard sale. I listened to him all of last Sunday morning. His voice is unequivocal in its quivering, just pure honest pain and suffering. Last week she found Gary Moore, not the comedian, but a British guitar player, who ranks up there with Eric Clapton and that guy who plays with Ten Years After. Can't remember his name. That happens when you get older, but I have the confidence and satisfaction that it will pop into my brain sometime within the next twenty-four hours. Gary Moore has one song that we played all day the first day we found him, "Still Got the Blues." If you don't know it, listen to it, hoping for you that you are with the one you love.

The next morning my brain released the name Alvin Lee to me. TheTen Years After guy. A shit eating grin tracked across my face. I had won again. Albert Alzheimer's was pushed into the back seat another day longer.

NEW LIFE

I OFTEN WONDER HOW this happened. We had known each other for at least two years and had spent many hours together with other folks. We always ended up sitting next to each other and talking, while others around us just disappeared from our singular cocoon. I would always kid about sex, what she liked, what the craziest sex she had ever had, etc. We would laugh, and she would roll her eyes like she was looking at a fan and punch me on the arm. Although we had a good time, our relationship was still in neutral position.

As time progressed our conversations started to converge on just us. We still talk about the line I used to get her to say yes to our assignation. I used it a multitude of times before it finally worked. It went something like this. "I miss more than anything having a smooth, warm female body next to mine. Would you let me come and get into bed with you, and we could cuddle and talk, nothing else, just that?"

She would always laugh and call me a dirty fat liar. "Oh no," I would protest mightily and we would giggle like we were fourteen years old. After one Friday night had ended on that familiar entreaty. I sat on my couch the following evening and drenched myself in the ever-increasing stupid inanity of modern television. I got a text message. "The answer is YES." What could I do but smile silently to myself? I texted back, see you in the AM. I was just too cool for school.

I went to her back door as always, and Katie opened the door. I had been in her house many times before but this was way different. She had a small kitchen, lots of wooden stuff. It was very clean and everything was in perfect position. The entire kitchen was dressed in granite counter tops, copper sinks, and a big black refrigerator. I remembered the time I had breakfast in her kitchen, and I noticed the black flatware we were using. I thought it very unusual that the forks matched her refrigerator. The silence of her house was always punctuated by the tinkle of wind chimes and soft music. I was devoid of any coolness. There was always the frail fragrance of vanilla in the air. I loved it. I still carry that smell with me when I leave her. It is the best.

I had always felt comfortable there. I didn't this time. We entered into, what can I call it, a very unpracticed awkward minuet. She looked at me and canted her head to one side. We kissed, then we kissed again, just to make sure. Next, we held hands and leaned against a counter top. The overhanging question was, who would jump off the cliff first? She assumed the lead and escaped off the ledge. She took me by the hand and said, "Let's bake some cookies."

The bedroom was an extension of her. Sophistication paired with comfort was a mirror of the lady who held my hand like she was leading a blind man.

Old people sex is an entirely different animal from young people sex and also middle-age people sex. Young people can have grade A sex in the middle of a nuclear attack, on a bed of nails, have it interrupted by a delivery from UPS and never miss a stroke. Middle-aged people can have sex on a wooden table top in the middle of a kitchen, only to have a car driven by a drunken school teacher crash through the living room wall. That'll maybe cause a brief interval, but then they'll retreat to the bedroom to top off the occasion. Old people require time, lots of time, preferred soft blues music, and concentration to the hilt. An occasional sexual fantasy doesn't hurt and understanding remains the most important ingredient of all.

These three levels of flight into the revelry of body sharing all are very different. It's hard to make a comparison. However, there is one constant that grows with age. The necessity of having both players who want the game to finish in a tie. The older you get the more conversation enters into the recipe for success. Foreplay sometimes becomes the only play and the most fun of all. Sex part names become part of the dialogue and once named they are permanently labeled. If the words,

Mr. Lucky or The Missus, happen to come up in this documentation, you should know that we are not talking about someone who just hit a scratch-off ticket.

You will have to be understanding in reading this, people in their seventies sometimes cannot keep pulling the same wagon of thought. It will vanish like a runaway teenager then come back after being gone for one night. Keep this fact in mind and be on the lookout for time warps or you might be led down a dirt thought road to absolutely nothing. It just evaporates or it might skip around like a gangly gamin.

See, I just did it., so let's go back to the Sunday morning.

Don't worry, I won't relate the gory details of the Jack and Katie junction. Just know that it was fun. On my side it was a tale of successful tantricular sex and for her it was a series of mountain top to mountain top explosions that never seemed to end. Afterwards, she sat straight up in the bed and sang softly to herself, I AM NOT DRY. Annie Lenox could not have done it better. Immediately I applauded and said "magnifique comme toujours." I don't speak French, so I hoped that meant very good. We both collapsed in the bed, laughing like two crooks who had just robbed a bank. The hook that remains in the closet of my mind is that it was like a road I had not been down before. It was like the two of us had been spiritually bound for a long time.

The next afternoon after our second successful coupling, we were putting on our clothes. I was slipping on my shoes. She said something about this not going anywhere and she was sure that pain was in the offing. As sure as autumn precedes December. I looked up at her and the following words came out of my mouth, "I love you too much to ever hurt you."

Startled does not suffice as a description of the reactions from both of us. I know what I felt. I felt like truth had been spoken. I was happy to have said it. She was more aware that this was not the normal practice for people of our age or any age for that matter. She was like a young girl on her first Ferris wheel ride. She liked it, but was not sure she wanted to continue to the end.

IN A TOWN CLOSE BY

KASEIN STOOD IN HER kitchen. She was preparing breakfast for her six-year-old daughter. Kasein was what her town folk would call a tall drink of water. Her hair was a robust strawberry blond with flecks of gold scattered like sparkles throughout. Music colored the entire room with sound. Kasein did a slow turn in time with the song and sang some of the words to herself. Her face was beautiful.

The music played second fiddle to the sound of Kalia as she danced into the room. She was a miniature of her mother, except for the freckles sprinkled across the bridge of her nose. The beauty had made a successful trip from mother to daughter.

"Mama, Happy Birthday. I made you a present. Try and guess what it is. You will never guess. I know you won't. You could guess for a thousand years and you would not get it. I will give it to you now.

Her hand came from behind her back in a flash. It held a picture drawn as good as any first grader could draw. It took Kasein a second to determine what it was. When she did her heart and head fell in love with Kalia one more time. It was a picture of her and Kalia holding hands and the words, *Just Us*, printed across the bottom in letters of all different colors and sizes.

ENTERING FROM
STAGE RIGHT

I AM INTRODUCING YOU to the crackerjacks in this box, sometimes one by one and sometimes in pairs. I will revisit the ones who you already know at another time.

The first official intro is Maryellen, librarian extraordinaire. She has all the trappings of a book minder. Mousy might be a little much, but you would never be burdened by carrying a picture of her around in your brain. If you were asked to describe her, you would be lost for details. I condensed a description of her down to this. Mary Ellen was a prototypical cataclysmic example of cosmic coincidence. Mary Ellen was a fuckin librarian, nuff said. She and Katie were best buddies. They talked and texted all the time. I sometimes would kid them about being library lezzies. Katie would sometimes stop in and talk with Maryellen; they would drink coffee and smoke fancy cigarettes. Then lie to me about that.

Her library was not one of those colossus libraries, but a very quiet suburban hideaway. Voices only carried the volume of a big whisper; coffee was always brewed and the aroma was totally a match for the surrounding environment. Maryellen was the perfect prefect. A person when first walking into the library would get the feeling of a soft warm cloak being draped around them. People talked with people they did not know, about things they did not discuss with others. It was a wonderful place to be.

Katie would lecture to me, the dullard uncool male, about friends.

As we were older, both of us had lost friends to cruel death and the previously mentioned Albert Alzheimers. She said that fast and true friends were to be nurtured, listened to, and taken care of. Overlook or just completely disregard character flaws. That means anything short of shop lifting underwear and sometimes homicide, if it was well deserved.

Physically, Maryellen had rust colored hair, invaded by sparse gray streaks, short but frizzy so that her head looked like a sunbaked spring dandelion. She possessed a big, big nose and a set of teeth that were V shaped from back to front. They projected out the front of her mouth, like a beak. They were covered by the Prometheus right above them. Katie did not like it if I said, "If not for Maryellen's nose her teeth would have a suntan." Body shape wise, she was a nine, it was like someone had constructed this great facility and then draped crappy ornaments all over it. I forgot to mention the titties. Small but shapely.

She was a widow in every direction. I had not known Enos due to his demise. His passing and my appearance on the scene missed crossing by a very short period of time. I wish I had, just so I could call him Enos the Penis, or ask him if he knew about Enos "Country" Slaughter, right fielder for the St. Louis Cardinals. Who once scored from first base on a single against the New York Yankees in the World Series...Did I mention that I am a Cardinals fan? Enos was followed by the most missfittable middle name in the history of mankind, Renoir. According to the photos I had seen, Enos looked like, from bottom to top, a half hard dick with eyes, ears, legs and arms.

From what I understand, Enos was a good guy. His reputation was under the extreme care of Ms. Maryellen. She loved Enos with a fierceness that burned like a steel furnace. She still fanned that flame with undiluted fervor after he took the long, long walk. It was great to watch this outwardly timid being become a lioness, roaring with passion upon the mention of Enos by anyone in which she detected a scintilla of negativity. Katie said when this transformation would occur, she would just sit in awe. Spittle would fly out of Maryellen's mouth and if you were standing in front of her you were glad for the moisture in that it might put out those unhinged flames coming out of her eyes.

Oft times, Katie and I talked about relationships and how the Maryellen/Enos liaison was a paragon that should be revered by everyone. As our union progressed, we would have long conversations delving into the potential juxtaposition with our doppleganging couple. The strength, the trust, the fun and laughter.

Anyway, back to Maryellen after the passing of Enos. The process of dying was not a hundred-yard dash. His illness dragged on forever and she was in attendance at each and every milestone. His last words were, "Remember, we are only half done." The story goes that he died in early morning and Maryellen did not call anyone for well into the afternoon. She could not stand the final separation, and you know who she called.

Katie told me of the many times that Maryellen spoke with her about that day. Maryellen said, that in her mind, there were long conversations throughout the entire passage between her and Enos. She held his hand almost the entire time. They talked about old times, good times, bad times, fucked up times, all good in the end. She said that she did not shed one tear. They agreed that they had been blessed to have each other and it would happen again. The house was completely devoid of any noise, the air did not move, everything had its place and all was good.

That day's construction was almost identical to other conversations that had occurred many times. They were both smiling and Enos was his usual goofball self. He kept saying, "It is time for me to go. My expiration date is way past due. I will start to smell of death. This conversation is going nowhere. God, I love you." Those words jumped into the air between them, not god I love you but God, (very strong), I love you (almost a whisper). It was a great way to die, with only the one you loved best at your side, Maryellen.

All of the above was Maryellen's reiteration of the death day morning and afternoon. It all carried the full weight of a familiar saying to me. "What a way to go."

This kind of happening, minus the death, occurred on a regular basis between Katie and me. We had that chain link connection. We were face to face, belly to belly spiritual souls, hooked up at the highest level.

Enough of this. Let's get on with the heart and guts of this story. This is a tale of two friends who shared a deep love with someone. No, it is not Katie and Jack nor Enos and Maryellen. It is Katie and Maryellen. Enos, could not speak for himself and Jack starts out as window dressing but steps up his contribution as things flow along. Just keep that in mind. Beans will be spilled in due fashion.

KATIE

THIS PART IS ABOUT Katie. Bear in mind, she is the Soul Conductor of my life and I love her with an intensity that I do not understand. It transcends any emotional plateau I ever considered possible. From day one I felt like I was sucked into a vortex of emotion that spits me out every day feeling like a suckled babe. I am reborn into a personage that breathes new fresh air all day, every day, everything I eat tastes just like it was supposed to taste. I know I am talking about me, but this is really about the settling she has forth from me. Katie was the most powerful, non- powerful person I have ever known.

Katie does not walk. She sashays. Every time she walks away from me a smile slides onto my face.

She loves music, so do I. Neither one of us are singers of professional talent, but we went out and bought ourselves a karaoke machine. We discovered that you could go on You Tube and bring up all kinds of songs that you could karaoke to. My favorite of all time is Greg Allman singing Queen of Hearts, only the rendition on the Laid Back album. I know that if someone else heard me singing that song it would precipitate much laughter and hooting, but I did not give one flying fuck. At that moment I was as good as it gets.

Katie has a quiet voice, but she can make me cry. I have tears in my eyes just telling you about it. It was absolutely wonderful. Two senior folks, sitting on the couch, semi in the bag, singing at least one quarter off key for hours.

Remember she is sixty five, she endured cancer prior to my appearance in her life, kicked its ass. She takes pills I don't question;

she is a believer in essential oils. She meditates every day, has terrible eating habits, smokes the occasional cigarette, has a very low tolerance of any alcohol, and she sports the most beautiful toes I have ever seen.

Her body was the body of a sixty-five-year-old female that was still in the original wrapper. Her skin was soft and smooth, like chiffon silk, her nipples were even smoother. There was only one contrast, her hands. They were working hands. Hands that knew strength and control. Hands that could give delectable strokes on one's backside and five minutes later drive a nail through a piece of Brazilian Ebony in minimum time. She loved sex, but it did not dominate her personality. She took it like breathing. It was part of her existence but it had its place and did not rule her in any way. Many times, we would just be doing stuff, talking about the weather, she loved weather stuff, eating a sandwich, reading the paper and we would start fooling around. Soft kisses, soft touches, it was sublime intimacy on display. It would last not too long, but just long enough, we called it sexual hors d'oeuvres. Always leaving room for the main course.

CHERIE

NOW ENTERING FROM STAGE left is the ever-effervescent Cherie Laveau. I am using that intro because Ms. Laveau was at one time a frontline stripper, displaying her wares to anyone with the proper currency. She is a close friend of both Katie and Maryellen. They formed an unusual triangle, with each occupying their third in good fashion without stepping on either of the others. Their triangle was in a constant state of flux, sometimes equilateral, sometimes isosceles and sometimes a scalene. Dependent on which of them was flaring the most. Maryellen was the anchor of most discussions and decisions, but the power shifted from one triangle to the other and sometimes coalesced into a stick figured house.

Cherie was slightly younger than the others, but it was an understood fact that she had more *street* experience than the other two. She had an arsenal of sex tools and could quote directions and describe the proper usage for all of them. Her favorite was the cockring.

I must jump in here and interrupt the Cherie introduction. I tried a cockring one time and only one time. I slipped it on, while sitting on the edge of a young lady's bed. I stood up to slide into the bed and the damn thing fell off onto the floor. That is not a good sign for the immediate bumping of uglies.

Cherie was by far the most outspoken one of the group. My favorite example of this was one day she was talking about Enos and said, "Enos could talk about anything from deification to defecation and never take one deep breath."

Katie started laughing at that. Without hesitation, Cherie punched a hole in her laughter, "Hold on to thyself, Ms. Katie, your guy has palaver as a main building block in his blood." Then she gave Katie an understanding smile that said, "And you know it."

Katie once asked Cherie why she started stripping, minus the money reason. Cherie gave a very succinct answer, "It was better than working in a sock factory." She drank more beer than anyone one I knew and peed more than any two pregnant women put together. She also claimed she had been smoking cigarettes since she was nine years old.

I am going to repeat a story Cherie told me one time. She and I had a great relationship in that we could tell each other deep down stories that were otherwise best kept wrapped up out of the light. The story goes like this. Cherie hooked up one night with this really young guy. She said that her cougar persona jumped the chain and was out of control. She could not remember his name, so we will call him Cletus, just for the hell of it. To make a long story short, they had consummated the dalliance and were taking a short smoke break. Cletus had that evil light bulb of remembrance start to glow above his head. He turned to Cherie and said, "I just remembered, my dad told me about you. You are Cherie the Stripper. He said you gave him a lap dance one night. Damn, I can't wait to tell him that he got the lap dance and I got the whole lap and attending features."

Cherie said she slapped the hell out of him, then said, "Your dad was a cheap son of a bitch, so get your clothes and get your boney ass out of here. Oh yeah, you got a little dick, it looks like a Vienna sausage. It doesn't even come close to shaking hands with the good spot."

Now she was creeping up on her tiptoes to the fifty mark. She was being slammed into the wall of "What am I gonna do now?" The demand curve for fifty-year-old strippers is not that steep and the sock factory was closed many years ago. She told me one day that it was like she was walking down a sidewalk and everyone else was riding by in a car. Futility filled her life, but, Cherie had one thing and I expect her to have it until at least three minutes before she dies. Cherie was sexy. Men looked at her and had lascivious thoughts, and it didn't matter if you were seventeen or seventy. She just had the look. She had teacup titties. As a matter of fact all three of them had "girls" that met that description.

You probably want a definition of these female china pieces. If you put two teacups on a table at just the right width apart, a woman that can bend over and has titties that would fall into the cups without any help at all. Those are teacup titties.

This description of reduced volume mammaries begs the question. How did Cherie get to be a stripper with below average bazooms? They usually did not fit the job qualifiers. The answer is that nobody ever looked above her waist. She had a magnificent ass. This attribute appeals to at least fifty percent of the world's male population. I have found that to be the absolute truth.

One of my best friends is a sworn-in member of what I call "Melonites." I fall on the side of being an ass man. I am not a man who needs his female companion to have wonderfully endowed melons. Responsive nipples are more important in the sexual process, if you know what I mean. Size is not that important.

Cheree had a man in her life. Trip was his name. He was a tall lanky person. He was one of those guys I just don't understand, in that he was one of those everyday handymen who could fix anything. It didn't matter if it was automotive, electrical, plumbing or just plain old carpentry. He could do it all and I stood in awe as I was restricted to screwing in lightbulbs. He dipped Copenhagen, and like all dippers, he continued to promise to quit on the next moon cycle or anything else that occurred on a regular basis.

He exuded confidence when presented with anything, except for Cherie. He seemed perpetually dumbfounded in her presence. He walked around her in stunned silence like she was a glistening bauble that he did not know how to polish.

Cherie in return, truly loved Trip. I think he was the only man she did not look at as a tool. A tool to be used and put away in a dark box until further usage was required. Cherie would never be looked at as a woman who had been rode hard and put up wet, but she could be described as a woman who might ride a man hard and put him up wet.

I think this slide show of Cherie should have given you a pretty good picture of this full-blooded woman.

JACK

I JUST REALIZED THAT I have not talked about Jack in the singular. I have not told you jack about Jack. Just to commend your inner Sherlock, you have probably come to the conclusion that I am Jack.

Yes, it is I. First of all, I have no lips, slight saddlebag looking things drooping down on each side of the nose, not Jimmy Durante size but not small. The late sixties did a number on me. Operations replacing and repairing stuff, permanent diseases moving into my body like unwanted stepchildren. I could feel senescent cells creeping through my body spreading evil shit all around. Sometimes I could feel myself fading into the shadows like the bass player in a rock and roll band.

HOWINEVER, I shall not give up. Every morning I wake up hoping to be blessed with a dick just hard enough for government work. I strive every day to snatch victory out of the jaws of defeat for another twenty-four hours. One of my heroes once said, "Hope springs a kernel, Denny Crane." I still have a lot of stuff to do. I continue to wait for the exact moment to sing to Katie, "Ahhh Sukie," just like Dwight sings it. I want to play the piano like Leon Russell or Don Shirley. Being the lead singer in a tight rock and roll band with three good looking black girls singing backup, (not racist, they are just better) would be dramatic. I want to drive a NASCAR hot rod, be able to throw a good pot, would like to run free just one more time, go to dinner at one of the original restaurants in Lyon, France, eat a hot dog in the left field bleachers in Wrigley Field. Oh yeah, one more big one, I would like to be Mike Trout for one day, but it would have to be in the middle of summer.

I have several very important questions to ask. How do fat people fuck? I mean really fat people. Have a really good explainer explain to me that electricity is not really magic. Why do people have cosmetic surgery, especially excessive cosmetic jobs so that their skin looks like a thrown away plastic bottle. I know the majority of people would say these are all small-minded things and they have no meaning. Probably right, but I really don't give a big rat fuck.

My demise is another thing of contention with my family. The first big surprise is going to be when they find out I spent all my money. The second gasp of surprise will be when they find out where my body goes when the slide for life ends.

There are seven body farms in the United States. These institutions allow you to have your remains laid out on the ground where they are allowed to decompose in a peaceful manner while being studied for criminology purposes.

I am going to one in Knoxville, Tennessee. First of all, it is free. They will come and get you if you live within one hundred miles. Second of all, it is a purposeful death. This probably is my only real contribution to society. I am not in a hurry to go there, but the thought of being burned up or put in an expensive box does not sit well with me. Besides, what if all the religious minions and super minions in the world are wrong, and you continue on into another world similar to what we have now? I will be free to go and the majority of you will have to go through some major repair work. That is what can truly be called the Last Laugh. Being laid out in the open sounds good to me. It is a necropolis with a view.

The absolute best thing that ever happened to me was Ms. Katie. Previously I have described our relationship from many sides. None of these could ever give you the true depth of our joining. Would it surprise you if I told you that we have never had but one argument? You could guess for thousands of eons and never guess it was about Neal Young. It only gave me a picayune pissed off. She likes him and I think he is probably the most overrated music person in the entire universe. Neal's vocal efforts evoke thoughts of small animals yelping. I am convinced his voice box is filled with nickels and you know, he IS from Canada. She likes him and says the usual in-folk disclaimers over how he is great writer, etc. etc., etc. plus yada, yada, yada. She has a permanent coupon which guarantees against any payback from me for that one failure.

Just this morning, we were talking and I told her that if anything ever happened to her, I would drown in sorrow, I would become a phantom. She chimed in with her "me too also" sentiments. This discussion led us to deciding that we would have to die together. Which led us down a twisted path of considering whether we should do one of those shoot your partner and then yourself dramas. We both agreed that we could not do that because neither one of us could shoot the other one and if we did then we would have to make the decision of whether that is really what we wanted to do. We do talk about some weird shit. I can only say that most relationships look like a landscape painting, while ours is a three- dimensional architectural model of how it should be.

So now, you know jack about Jack.

Oh yeah, there is one more thing. I only have somewhere between now and one year to live. Two weeks ago, I had a ninety day visit to my doc. After the usual test barrage, he sat down and looked me straight in the eye. I could not help it, I laughed. Whenever I looked at him, I could only think of Joe Walsh on a smaller scale.

"Jack, you and I have been friends for at least twenty years now, since I first moved to town as a young smartass doctor. I wish I did but, I do not have good news. Your heart is in the bottom of the ninth, with one out, an 0-2 count on your weakest hitter and nobody on base." The doc lowered his head as if he was looking for words that might have been dropped on the floor by someone else, breathed a partial breath and continued. "At this point, I cannot give you exact time parameters, but you have to see me on a monthly basis. You should get your affairs in order. Your body will start to give signals and you should take them as truth. I do not want to mislead you to expect a turn in this diagnosis. I would not have had this conversation without already having gotten a backup opinion. I wish I could give you better news. Giving advice in this situation is not something I am able to do. You will need to lean on your closest friends and it is up to you on what you want to tell them. Do you have any questions for me?"

Do you remember when you were riding your first bicycle? A

hard fall happened and you had the breath knocked out of you. That is close to what I felt like. I could not get my breath for what seemed like a small forever.

I did know not what to do. Does someone in my position cry? It might come later, but not now. The movie that showed on my brain screen was like one of those television screens where you watch about six or seven different sporting events at once. What do I do, do I tell anyone? The doc had talked to me like he was going over the details of a sad happening. Not like he was pinning a death notice on my forehead. I had shit to do. First of all, I had to get my ass out of his office.

"Well damn, doc. I kinda wish you had sugarcoated that a little bit. I don't have any thoughts at all at this moment. Can I call you tomorrow after I have had a little digestion time with this?"

He gave me his card and wrote his cell number on it. "Call me anytime, if I am busy, I will get back to you as soon as I can."

I think I said thanks and walked out. I really don't know.

I sat in my car for a while, I don't know how long. All of my life whenever something bad happened to me, my first reaction was to start thinking of how I could overcome that trouble or at least fight with it. Every single time. This was different. I could not do battle. I was going to lose no matter what. I felt like Napoleon on his boat trip to Elba. Surely worse.

I had this thought. One of my friends who had just been diagnosed with cancer told me, "Jack, when you tell someone you have cancer, they never look at you the same again." In that moment, I made a decision not to tell anyone, because from that moment on I would not be treated like Jack. I would be treated with kid gloves and soft words. No one would have the balls to tell me to "Go jump up a goat's ass." or call me a "pencil dicked motherfucker." That would be the worst. No one will know, including Katie. I want my last days to be as good as possible. I want Jack to be treated like Jack and not Jack with the accoutrement of death. I could not see light at the end of the tunnel, but at least I now had a tunnel. I could not be a poltroon.

The ride home was very strange. I had the hunger for music. I don't know all I listened to but I do know I listened to 'Wish I Knew You When I Was Young'.

Let's get on with this story, my death should be put in the back seat, after all that is where Hank Williams died.

GETTING TO RENFROE

LATE ONE WEDNESDAY AFTERNOON at the office of Renfroe Rooks.

The phone on the desk rang twice, was picked up and answered. "Rooks Law Office, this is Arlene."

"My name is Kasein Russell, I would like to make an appointment with Mr. Rooks. Tomorrow at 4:00. Is that possible?"

"May I ask the nature of you request?"

"I would like to discuss a matter of family law with Mr. Rooks."

"Could you be more specific?"

"No, not at the present. Look lady, I do not want to take up a lot of time with Mr. Rooks, I have some questions that need answers. I have done my homework and he is particularly suited to answer those questions. I do not want to talk with another attorney."

"Ms. Russell, we will see you tomorrow at 4:00."

The next day Kasein listened to 'Down from the Mountain Top' by Ian Noe on the way to Panama City and tried to rinse the remains of the day from her mind. Some days when she was in her classroom, she felt like a scarecrow in a garden of dandelions. On those days her job seemed like a fruitless employ.

She entered the city limits and her thoughts centered on her appointment with Renfroe Rooks. It was important that she not screw this up. Kasein knew that Mr. Rooks was a good friend of Jack Riordan and was his former law partner. She hoped that he was the definition of avuncular and would understand her request.

A FRIENDS SADNESS

IT RIPPED KATIE'S HEART out by the strings to be with Maryellen. She had always enjoyed their tete a tetes. They fixed so many problems, they steered clear of things that they could not control, i.e. economy, world peace, toe nail fungus. Their conversation ranged far and wide and was unencumbered with the usual boundary lines of human discourse. All thoughts carried currency to spend in advancing a theory. It didn't matter whose idea it was or how far it stretched the balloon of believability.

I think that Maryellen took Katies staunch belief in essential oils with a grain of Frankincense. However, she would never cross the river of sarcasm to dig at Katie about her conviction of success in using those oils and pills.

In turn, Katie kept opinions to herself when it came to the goodness of mankind in general. Deep in her heart, Maryellen believed that given a decent opportunity, things like socialism would work simply because everyone would share and share alike. Kate's opinion in that regard is that it all would end up in a giant clusterfuck of universal economic enemas.

This all changed with the passing of Enos. Sorrow had walked into their relationship wearing pointy toed cowboy boots. Stomping all joy out of the patois created by Maryellen and Katie. The air of glee and laughter had been sucked out of all their rooms.

Katie had a minor explosion one day, approximately one year from Enos's departure. It went something like this. "Maryellen, please oh please talk to me about Enos. I miss him too. I want to know what it was like to be in the Maryellen/Enos union." At that very moment, Maryellen had raised her coffee cup to her lips, she came to a complete stop, she was a still photo. She did not move for what seemed like a long time. She slowly lowered the cup into its saucer and it sat there, still, until a tear tore the surface of the liquid. That tear was the finger removed from the dike; her face shattered like a broken egg shell. The words poured forth, not fast, unhurried, but steady as an old clock.

"Mornings are the worst. I would always lay in the bed after Enos got up. The same thing happened every day. I would roll over to his side of the bed, still warm and his personal smell would wrap me like a dense fog. It would be all I could do not to roll around and giggle. Those moments might be the apex of my joy. Enos would be clattering around in the kitchen. I would go forward with my morning ministrations; brush teeth, pee, fool around with my hair. My nightly uniform was a pair of baggy, soft pajama bottoms and one of Enos' old white tee shirts. He claimed that was the sexiest thing I could ever wear.

"From this point on, there was no standard routine. Enos might slide into the room and sneak up behind me while I was brushing my teeth, slip both of his hands inside my shirt and softly caress my small titties. He was a nut about those titties. On a scale of one hundred, this action was only about a ten in the realm of sex. It was just affection, just something he liked to do. Or, he might come back into the bedroom carrying the Bluetooth with Boz Skaggs singing, 'Lowdown', one of the most danceable tunes ever. Enos would be doing this funky dance that he and he alone owned. He would be leaning slightly back from the waist up, arms extended, doing some wavy motion with his elbows. He just knew he was a sexy fool when he did this. The most it ever got him was a smile on my face. Well, not always. Sometimes there would be a swerve into the sex curve."

Maryellen took a small sip of her coffee and jumped back into her dialogue.

"I know that I will never get to cut his toenails again and have him demand that I speak Vietnamese. I guess that was better than having to put on a nurse's dress or the uniform of a young girl's boarding school.

"Did you know that Enos considered himself an undiscovered songwriter? He had this song, 'Nekkid Dancin,' that he had been writing since the night we first made love. Twenty years later, he had one verse that he was happy with, he had no sense of music other than he loved it, here is the one verse."

Days into days, years into years.
All woven into a basket of lonely tears.
Baby, you are right and I am so wrong.
Take me to bed and sing me a song.
We be nekkid dancin the whole night long.

"The strange part to me was when he was away from me, he morphed into the accountant whose name he carried with aplomb. No one in his business coterie had any idea what an absolute nut job he was. I had observed him many times in the business suite. He was on top of his game in all situations. He could provide well-crafted solutions to problems that had been given up on by others. His personality was capable of knowing when to quit and when to bow up like a cornered boar hog. His intelligence was extraordinary and his integrity would not crack no matter how big the dollar amount that hung in the balance. Once the tie came off, it was always and only Enos and Maryellen. His whole being was Enos and Maryellen. We were paramount in his life.

"He and I knew that if we were in a crowd, no one would notice us. It was like we were two puffs of smoke. If we happened to come face to face with an acquaintance at a party, we could maintain idle chatter until that person just had to go across the room to say hello to a long-lost friend. We did not care one whit because we had the answer that was unknown to most pairs. We had the perpetual umbilical connection that allowed us to be anything and everything to the other."

Maryellen took another break, just as a smile flowed across her face as if she just remembered a better time.

"One of my favorite things was for Enos to get sick. I don't mean the killer sick, just something like a mild flu bug. It gave me the opportunity to take care of just him, he would let me boss him around, make him take pills and give him a massage. I often accused him of going into houses where there was a lot of kids, in hopes that he might come down with something.

"He would use words of yore in the midst of sex. He would raise himself up on his hands and tout himself in loud voice, 'I am bestride a young damsel in distress and shall slay many dragons as recompense for this mountainous moment in my life.' The only problem with that is that we would laugh too much which would cause coitus collapse, a non-communicable disease. Thank God for that. Good god, Katie, you let me rattle on for a good half hour."

Maryellen got up from the table and walked across the room and fiddled with her Bluetooth and Lowdown started to pulse forth from the speakers. Her demeanor spoke of total emptiness. Maryellen looked at Katie like she was looking for a savior.

"Katie, would you dance with me?" And they danced.

Katie felt drawn to something as if she was a random nail being drawn to a magnet. It was not clear yet, but she was surely being pulled through the bulrushes of decision. She could not quite grasp it as it floated around in her head, but she felt peace as if she were being lifted and lain onto a soft bed. It was coming, she knew it, like a jigsaw puzzle that was half done. You could see a partial picture but you could not be certain of what the end would be.

Katie asked, "Do you still miss him? I don't mean as a companion. I mean as a lover. Do you have a visceral ache for him to put his hands on you? I know we are old, but Jack and I stay fully engaged with that part of our lives and if he were gone, I would feel feeble and wrinkly all over. I have this theory that it keeps me smooth and breathtakingly beautiful." Heh, heh, like she was still the Queen of the Hop.

Maryellen looked at Katie over the top of her coffee cup. "I miss that more than anything, every night we would go to sleep in the proverbial spoon alignment. He would always whisper in my ear something silly, like, 'Baby, in a deep movie star voice, if during the night you feel prodded from behind, don't be scared, it will only be Dr. Dooright wanting to start up a conversation with the Missus."

Maryellen looked up and half smiled as only a fond remembrance could cause. "His hands had the ability to glide over my body with a silken grace. He would combine this with kisses that started on my mouth and then he would scatter them like warm raindrops over my whole body. He was a man who wanted to make his woman a happy child. No one won, we both did."

Maryellen felt like a seventy- eight record that had gotten to the center part, the record was still going around but no sound came out. She was done.

RUMINATIONS

KATIE PONDERED, AM I wrong or do I feel like Jack and I were part of a relationship parallelogram. Were Enos and Maryellen our Doppelganging other halves. It was not physical. Maryellen was short, Katie was tall, Jack was tall, Enos had been kind of roundish. It was an alignment of souls.

She started to do a mental comparison chart. Enos definitely fell on the funny side of life. So did Jack. Both a smidgen off center. Both took looks at life from different angles. Enos worked on writing a song for years. Jack just had a title that he loved to tell people about just to get a reaction. "I'd commit suicide but it's too much trouble to be born again." He called it the first country and western song about reincarnation, although I understand that Ray Wylie Hubbard went through a period of brief involvement with reincarnation and wrote a song about wild horses that was supposed to be about that subject. Or it might have been a sideways jab at the God folk. I didn't know much about Enos and his take on spirituality, certainly not on religion. Jack was highly suspicious of religiosity. He blamed it on his being raised in the Baptist church. Katie knew she could go on and on about Jack's stance on God and such. He said that the dogma of Christianity was way, way off. That it totally eliminated the possibility that God had a sense of humor or that he dealt in fairness.

He thought that there should be a book of cuss words that explained the origin and meaning of each one, example; what is the difference between skat and shit. He could go off on his specialty by discussing the universally despised cuss word, Goddamn, which he said actually was a phrase, God Damn.

"God Damn", according to Jack, "Should not be looked at as taking God's name in vain. In the first place his first name is probably not God. In the second place, if he was the great God on high, God Damn should be looked at as the best damn you could put forward. You don't hear anyone saying 'COW DAMN.' It is a compliment that you used his name to damn someone. You came with your best."

Jack continued, "I have this vision that when I die, I will be at the office of decision. There will be a long line of desks, sitting behind each desk will be this person dressed in a white robe with two big switches on the desk that said UP and DOWN. Long lines would be in front of each desk. I was shuffled into a line along with a bunch of other people...Young, old, black, white, all races, sexes and ages represented. I got to the front of the line and expected the guy to ask me for my Social Security number. But, the desk guy said, "Jack, sorry to give you the bad news but you are going down." Then he said "Next." And motioned me to the left where an elevator like thing awaited my arrival.

All at once a loud voice overrode all noise in the room, "Hey, isn't that the guy who had the only correct usage of God Damn. He understood that it could be used in vain OR it could be used as a valid instrument of rebuke. He was capable of not just accepting the authority and interpretation of a bunch of old farts from long ago... Isn't your name Jack? I am Jimmy God. Turn around and get on the escalator to Heaven. Have a nice eternity. We have good baseball up here, all year long. Ha Ha."

Jack would discontinue this rant, turn on his heel and say "Think about it."

Katie would take all of this and mind ramble through all of the mental rubble, but kept coming back to Maryellen's sorrow. The tears that perched on her lower eye lids when she spoke of Enos. She wondered if the roles were reversed would she speak of Jack in those hallowed tones. She hoped she would never have to answer that question.

A soft parachute landed and delivered to Katie a solution to the conundrum she was dealing with and, Katie breathed deep and felt good.

That night she lay in bed with Jack beside her. They both lay on their backs and stared at the ceiling. Jack rolled over to face Katie and said, "O.K. what's up my luscious girlfriend? What is the dilemma we are faced with?" He always used the pronoun we; it was never mine or his, it was ours "Baby, it is not ours to bear, let's play a game."

Katie immediately put her fist up to her face to create an ersatz mic and pronounced in a deep voice, "The major question for tonight's contest is the following: what is the worst way for someone to express their love?" Jack raised his hand as if he was in the in the third grade. Katie called on him in her best teacher voice. "What is your bid for the 'Championship of Worst Way to Express Your True Love?" His answer caused Katie to turn over to face the wall and feign sleep. Jack wins hands down. All other contestants would have walked away.

His answer, "I love you so much I am constipated."

A distinct whisper came from the person facing the wall, "Jesus, he is a sick man but the man I choose to do good work."

The balloon was in the air.

FIRST STEPS WITH RENFROE

KASEIN WALKED UP THE stairs, at the top was a large man with a kind face. She knew this was Renfroe Rooks. As she got closer, he spoke in a voice that was totally devoid of asperity. "Come on in, young lady. Have a seat and I will be right back."

His office spoke only of Renfroe Rooks Big comfortable leather chairs, a desk that could only be described as an expanse. Family pictures and none of him with a governor or some other panjandrum. No deer heads or dead fish on the walls. All business but in amenable terms.

He returned to the room. Sat down and leaned back in his chair, all the while looking at her as if trying to decipher her reason for being there. Renfroe sat up and placed his hands on his desk and said, "What can I do for you? Most of my clients are old men trying to finagle themselves out of something that was starting to be unpleasant. You are a welcome surprise."

"Mr. Rooks."

He interrupted, "Call me Renfroe."

"Renfroe, my name is Kasein Russell. My mother, Linda Russell, died one year and four months ago. It was a lingering demise. During that period, she called me one afternoon and asked me to come over."

"Arlene should have told you that I am not an expert on family law." Kasein blew that interruption off like it never existed.

MARYELLEN'S DILEMMA

MARYELLEN LAY IN BED; another day of melancholia lay ahead of her like a long stretch of highway. But, this time, she thought of all the people in her life that she had lost over the years. The child she never knew, stillborn, but she knew it was a girl, a beautiful flower that never had a chance to blossom. One parade she never got to walk in. Motherhood. Many times, Maryellen wondered how she would have worn that cloak. She gave herself an A minus, too much love and not enough discipline. All of those things she would never know.

Those thoughts took her in a straight line to Annabelle, her mother. She had been a lady of great intelligence and grace. She was a school teacher, and still today, Maryellen would have people come up to her in the grocery store and ask if she wasn't Annabelle's daughter. Then they would tell her that her mother had taught them in the 4th grade and what a great teacher she was.

Annabelle played the piano in the church for many, many years and I still remember the only time she gave the appearance of being flustered. The church bought an organ, which was another animal altogether to play. She stewed about this for a long time but my father stepped up and did what I still consider one of his greater deeds. He had an organ delivered to our house. Annabelle practiced that thing to death. She became an accomplished organist and made a grand debut one month later. I guess all of us have vignettes that they remember of their childhood and one of my favorites of my mother was her playing the Saint Louis Blues with me sharing the piano bench beside her.

My father departed this earth first, but he was something. You could never get your mind wrapped around him. He only went to eight grades in school, but in my mind, he was extremely smart. Not very affectionate, except with my mom. He loved baseball. I still remember driving all over town at night, looking for a spot where he and I could listen to KMOX and our beloved St Louis Cardinals. He was a short man with a big belly, had asthma and could not see out of one eye. I never knew why but he always fastened his belt on the left side not in the middle like everyone else. He could really sing, almost one of those high lonesome tenors.

Now I don't have Enos. I am alone, except for Katie and I guess I could count Jack as a perimeter friend. Everyone has people around them, but the ones that count are your intimate friends. The ones that know everything and sometimes way too much.

I have to get up and push the string of life a little bit more. Katie called and wants to have breakfast. It must be something earth shaking. She wants to go out to breakfast, while we usually just meet at one of our houses, very curious. Katie has been in a slump as of late, she is burdened like a mine donkey, carrying a heavy unseen load in the dark.

Every day I look for signs that might signal the end of the long, long Enos death tunnel. Nothing provides even a teeny tiny sparkle. Everything I do is gray, there are no bright colors.

I should change his name to Enos Everything. His non-presence leaves a tincture on all things. It doesn't matter if it is a moment of despair or just not having a shared cup of coffee in the morning. It is like all the planets are revolving around the sun named Enos. A dining room table becomes a tableau that features Enos and me. In quiet conversation about our mortgage payment and whether we should re-finance or not. The refrigerator door opening provides a light showing Enos opening it in the dark of night looking for something to share with me in bed. Toast and jelly was his favorite. We would sit nekkid in the blackness and eat jelly toast. We called it jelly to belly toast points.

Sitting at a stop light, would bring forth my man acting like a drag racer in our very tame hybrid car. He would briefly glance at the driver next to us and then do a vertical twirl with his forefinger, like he wanted to wind it up for a race. When the other guy would take off, Enos would throw up his hands like something was wrong with his car. Then laugh like hell. Like I said, he was a nutcase.

It had been a year now and I could not describe myself as a glass half full or a glass half empty. I felt I wasn't even a paper cup. Dismal, I am dismal.

THE PROPOSITION

TODAY HAS A SLIGHT change. I am going out to breakfast with my best friend. Katie wants to meet at her new favorite eatery. It was a combination of being a retro, modernistic, hippy health food café. You could get anything there. A person would be so healthy eating a spinach leaf and cheese omelet made with eggs that came from chickens that had never stepped on concrete and only ate blue corn. How about a smoothie made only from ingredients that were red, blue or green, a combination which made it look like mud? My favorite was the bowl with chia seed pudding as the foundation for all sorts of berries.

Katie floated through the door like an effeminate Aladdin. She had on what I called her work uniform. Dark slacks, matching jacket, open collared shirt with small pin stripes of aqua versus white.

Quite striking and totally incongruous with the flipped-out girl I knew who once painted her alternating toe nails black and white. This made her toes look like piano keys. She said Jack liked them and he would sit down by her feet, play air-piano and pretend he was Leon Russell playing "Stranger in a Strange Land". He would break into song with "How many days has it been since I was born, how many days till I die." He would hesitate and point at her, and Katie would become the three backup singers singing "Stranger in a strange land, stranger in a strange Land". Jack's singing was a combination of a yelp and a howl.

When Jack was not around, she would say, "If you combine those two things into a sound then you could call it HELPING." Katie was good with portmanteaus.

Katie slid into the chair next to mine. "We always sat that way because we could whisper when we did not want to share our conversations with the common folk. She was radiant as if she had showered in shiny water. Something had changed, something was afoot. I could feel it in the air like rubbing your fingers on corduroy.

"Have you ordered yet?" Katie asked.

"Of course not," I replied.

"Two coffees, straight up," we ordered simultaneously.

"Ok", I asked, "What is it? Did Jack bring home some new sexual deviation unbeknownst to all but him? Did you win the mega lotto? Did you figure out how to screw some bad guy out of his money? What is it that has stemmed the tide of despair which you have worn like an overcoat for the past few months?"

"No, my child," Katie whispered in a veiled voice. "It is all about Miss Maryellen. By the way did I tell you I invited Cheree to join us?"

As if on cue, the former sock maker appeared at our table and took the seat across from me. I had the feeling that the seating was significant, two against one. Cheree bubbled forth," Good morning Maryellen and Katie, the other two members of my life triangle. In addition to that fact, this morning is gonna be damn good, and I am not talking about the food."

We ordered; I went with the chia seed pudding. Both of the others went for the pancakes with ricotta cheese and lush warm maple syrup. While we waited, we bantered about silly things. Nervous chatter was a better description. The waitress served the food quickly and quietly with a quizzical look on her face, as if she knew she was in dangerous waters. Without a riposte from anyone, all three of us daintily plunged into the repast as only three mature women can do. A small sinister dirigible of quietness hung over the table. First one word, then another began to splat onto the tablAe. Good, scrumptious, mighty fine. I had inhaled enough of this intrigue.

"What have you two manipulative bitches come up with now?" I asked.

Cheree promptly cried out, "Not me, I am only here as a mediator. To make decisions of judgement, to provide definitions. A peacekeeper as it were." She without hesitation threw Katie under a big vehicle. "Not none of me. She is the parent of this dealie."

I slowly turned my head to the left and said, "Proceed, young lady." And proceed she did.

"Maryellen, you know that you are my sister from another mother, in the best way. We did not arrive on this earth having slid down the same love canal to become natural sisters. We chose each other as a BFF and in my mind that makes us stronger and better sisters. Based on this foundation, I had delivered out of the universe to me a poultice for your sorrow. It will be like the bright sliver of sunshine that sometime comes in the middle of a rainy day. It is not designed to completely erase the sorrow and is not meant to. It is a temporary respite from an eternal condition. What I am going to propose will require you to take deep breaths and unlock your mind for extreme expansion. I have thought long and hard about this presentation and I am perplexed as to whether I should just blurt it out and then explain or vice versa. Do you have a preference?"

"No," was Maryellen's answer.

"Blurting it is, Maryellen, I think you should sleep with Jack. Not often, but seldom would be acceptable. I am good with that. What do you think?"

Katie, moved slightly away from the table as if getting ready to run.

Maryellen just stared straight ahead as if she was a hand carved statue.

The area around the table had no sound, not even breathing. It was almost painful. The short time seemed like a minor eternity. Coffee immediately turned cold and could not be reheated. People within ten feet looked away. The food was totally forgotten. It was great theater.

After a minute or two or three, Maryellen slowly swiveled her head to the left and spoke directly to Katie. "Are you out of your fuckin' mind? Have you completely left the planet? Do you know what you have done? You have changed our entire paradigm and it can never be repaired. Just what was your reasoning to even suggest something like that to me? Your sister, yeah, just tell me which road you went down to arrive at this deviant address."

Sarcasm dripped from her voice like a faulty faucet. The words came out of her mouth like spit.

Katie hesitated and the air stood still and the coffee got colder.

Katie after a brief pause gathered herself and said. "Well, it all sprung from my recognizing that our two relationships bore a great similarity. Great deep love, tenderness and understanding. Our relationships when stripped of the physical stuff were reflections of one to the other. In an old southern expression, the relationships were side by each. I have always known this. Many times, during our conversations I would have a feeling of déjà vu. The interactions of our congresses were almost identical. The feelings you expressed toward Enos were the same things I said about Jack. This was not a five-minute idea, I have placed this idea in the middle of my mind room and mentally walked around it many, many times, trying to consider all the ramifications of this arrangement. I refused to infuse the concept with pop slang, like Friends with Benefits or One Night Stand. This was one friend seeing another friend in the midst of dire straits and wanting to pull her from the black water. I think you should consider Jack a revenant, a connection between you and Enos."

If this was a romantic novel, the phrase, "She wrung her hands," would be appropriate.

Maryellen continued to look at Katie with tear filled eyes. She turned and asked of Cheree, "What do you think of this?" The answer came quickly, "I am not a good person to ask that question. I have always wanted to do Jack, so my answer would be shaded by lust. My unbiased answer would be, it can't hurt anymore to think about it. Katie has already thrown the rock through the window, so now it is up to you to concur or not. The two of you are quite unusual and if it was anyone else, I would dismiss it as drivel out of hand. But honestly, I just don't know. The only ground rule I would like to impose is that the one thing that should remain untouched is your relationship with Katie and that ground rule may make it unlikely that you should follow through."

Maryellen slowly shook her head as if soft breezes were blowing her head back and forth.

"I have promised myself many times that I would do anything to preserve my friendship with Katie, but promises are sometimes like my mother's pie crust. They crumble quickly. What does Jack think about this?"

Katie spoke very slowly. "Jack doesn't know, I did not have the emotional energy to go through it with him without your approval. I have no idea what he would say." Confidence had run from her voice like a frightened gazelle.

Maryellen, slowly came out of her seat to full height and uttered the following. "Katie, I shall love you until my last breath, but I think I should go now." She slowly walked out the door without looking back. Her spoken phrase just did not tell the whole story. A vacuum had been created and the entire room was as silent and cold as an early Saturday morning morgue. Something had shifted the earth on its axis into a new tilt.

COGITATION

I HAVE NO RECOLLECTION of the drive to my house. I felt like I had gone through a shape shifting while still in the same body. What right did Kate-somehow the name Kate was better than Katie at this juncture-have to disrupt my sorrow and grief with a cockamamie, no pun, scheme like she proposed this morning. Totally asquare with my mood, I suddenly was hungry and remembered that I had left my chia pudding barely touched. What to do? What to do? Eat a big bowl of oatmeal and then brace the decision of whether to even consider Kate's ersatz conjugal visits or toss it out like last night's bed pan. I don't know how I came up with this approach to Kate's proposal. That decision of consideration or not had to be put to bed before even considering the pros and cons of using Jack as a psychological potion.

Consternation was my first mental position. Why had Kate done this? Where did it come from? Had I signaled like a third base coach that I needed male companionship in a connubial fashion? Of course, during the last year, upon occasion, I said, "I just need to get laid." But it was always couched in humor. Did she have a hidden agenda or did she put this forward as an honest forthright suggestion solely for my benefit. All of these things raced through my mind as I ate my oatmeal, which had been prepared the same way since I was nine years old. Oatmeal, brown sugar and butter on top, eaten after the butter melted.

Many thoughts entered my brain and flew around inside like a host of hummingbirds. It was not possible to follow all of them. I have always been able to take a situation and peel the onion layer by layer, to get to the heart of the matter. But this damn onion was too big. I could not get my cranium matter to flow around this fandango. It was too off the wall for my brain to react. I was still in emotional shock from the very moment she said those seven words, "I think you should sleep with Jack."

Had I ever entertained the idea of entertaining Jack in a sexual manner? Be honest, Maryellen. Be very honest. Well, maybe a little, but not in a manner that would cause me to ever really do it. Jack and I had always maintained a strictly platonic relationship. Hugs were never full body hugs. They always had that slight turn so that we entered the hug at forty-five-degree angles and never stayed there too long. You can tell if a person is crossing that fine line, and that never happened.

The real relationship was always between Kate and me. Jack and Enos were not exactly decorative or just car drivers, but they knew their place within the best friend's dynamic. Kate and I had often bragged to each other how our males never entered the evil realm of jealousy towards either one of us. They seemed to be proud of their strong, independent women. Now as I think about it, Kate and I were proud of them, although it was a little different as Enos left the building prior to the appearance of Jack.

A small slither of understanding Kate's proposition crept out from under the rug as I remembered how Jack always seemed at the ready to make me happy. Happy with Kate, happy with my food, making sure I could see at a ball game and was not behind the foul pole. I remember one time that he made Kate swap seats with me so that I could see better. It did not bother Kate one iota. She was the least interested person in athletics that I had ever known.

For the first time that day, I felt an easy smile ease onto my face as I revisited the time that I had tried to explain four downs to make a first down to Kate. It took a good thirty minutes and ended with my saying, "Just look at that guy holding a pole on the sideline and look for the number on the pole, that will tell you what down is next."

Maybe, just maybe that attitude that caused Jack to treat me that way was the genesis of Kate's solution for sorrow. Maybe, just maybe, she grasped that small spark and fanned it into a major flame. Maybe, she recognized Jack's concern for my emotional mud as a tunnel out of my darkness, as something that could fill the lacuna created in my life by the passing of Enos. Maybe, she believes Jack could supply something in my life that to him was a parallel action to moving me from behind a foul pole at a baseball game.

She had to have had a shitload of trust in both of her friends. Actually, it was a very courageous decision to offer your one and only soul link to someone else. I knew Jack had participated in something similar many years back.

One night when he was a little drunk, (truthfully, we were all a little drunk), he told us that one night he took a call from a girl he run into a couple of times. She was an acquaintance at best. She quickly got to the point. She had a friend, Linda. Jack did not know Linda at all, but Linda was well aware of Jack. Linda's birthday was the following Friday. The present she requested for herself was that she could be with Jack that night. This all was spilled out to Jack without any introductory massage. The question followed: Jack, would you be that present?

His usually clunky self said, "Do I have to wear a bow?"

"No bow," said the girl whose name he could not remember, "Just show up at the Dockside bar around seven and we shall see what we shall see, it goes where it goes." Jack, being the dog, he was, agreed. The entire phone call was all of one minute. He hung up and said to himself, "What the hell." We did not get the dirty details other than he and Linda ended up skinny dipping in a trailer park swimming pool. The skinny dipping led to the next ten days of sex, alcohol and rock and roll. Jack said they never got around to last names and one day they both just knew it was time to walk away. Besides, Renfroe wanted him to come back to work.

Jack swears that was the last time he ever saw his swimming partner except when he was at a New Year's Eve party and ran into her and her husband. She acted like Jack was an old friend and that was that. Kate and I gave him hell and said that the abrupt ending of the coital adventure must have meant he never quite measured up to his reputation. He denied it all and maintained his studly performance was in the top fifteen percent of studly performances. Jack said, this was just further proof that he was a giver not a taker, besides this was not last week. It was a long time ago. What would he do now with his wife's best friend? Had libido laziness encrypted Jack to bow out of anything that dropped into this arena.

The balance of the day was a blur, I can't remember a thing I did all day long, just sat and rehashed the hash being offered to me. This was all very strange to me. Before, when presented with some type of gordian knot, the first thing I would do would be to call my best friend and confidant. You know who, well, that bandaid had been ripped off at breakfast this morning.

SURPRISE BY KASEIN

KASEIN SAT FORWARD IN the chair, "I know what your practice is, I am not here to talk about contracts and deeds. I am here on a personal matter and according to my research, you are the one best positioned to give me some advice. I am willing to pay.

"Jack Riordan is my father. He does not know that I exist. He also has a granddaughter that is six years old, Kalia. This is the revelation my mother gave to me on that afternoon she had me come over to her house. It was one of her last afternoons. She knew that death was in transit to her house and she said the same thing I just told you. Apparently, she and Jack had a torrid affair that only lasted about two weeks or so. She had been a phantom admirer of his for a long time. Her best friend took it on herself to ask Jack to show up for my mother's birthday outing and be presented as a present to mom. This led to a two-week scrimmage between Jack and my mother. I am the result. My mom married and John Russell had always been my father. He passed away about five years ago.

"Mr. Rooks, there are two things I have to make crystal clear for you.

"I know that Jack Riordan is my father. I stalked him for about three days off and on and finally followed him into the hot dog stand on Harrison Avenue. Kalia and I sat across the room from him and I got to observe him for a good while. There are physical traces, but the clincher was when he got up, I went over and confiscated the cup he had been drinking from. The DNA test confirmed that I was the product of the Jack and Linda tryst.

"The first thing is that I have no intention of disrupting Jack's life or have any financial designs on him at all.

"Secondly, the purpose of my meeting with you is that my one desire is for Jack to meet his granddaughter and with some luck, they come to know each other as grand relatives. You see, Mr. Renfroe, I have a heart problem and my life has no guarantees on longevity. I am looking to you for advice how I might advance this effort and possibly use you as an introductory pathmaker.

MARYELLEN AND THE DEATH DAY

SOMEHOW MY MIND TOOK me back to the day Enos died and the time we spent the rest of that day, him dying and my talking. The weather was not death weather. It was a day I shall never forget. Not the dying part, but the feeling I had just sitting there holding his hand. The feeling was a combination of his being gone and that he would never be gone from me, he would be with me forever.

I could feel myself wrapping my arms around the concept that Kate could become Katie again in my brain. I love Katie as one should love a friend. She would not hurt me for anything, at least not on purpose. So, I am going now to take the next step and consider the concept itself, the pros and cons, the ramifications of the experiment, for that is what it was. I could feel myself being drained like a kitchen sink and I could do nothing more except go to bed.

The re-clothing process took place and, yes, I still wore one of his old white tee shirts and soft flannel bottoms. Just in case he should show up again. But, I could not rid myself of the dying day. A part of the conversation returned to me as clear as if had been etched with a diamond bit. It went like this. Enos saying to me, "Baby, you are a young lady, I want you to have a happy, full life. If you find someone who you love and want to spend the rest of your life with, I understand and would support your decision with one caveat. Immediately and I mean immediately when you enter the dead life, you drop that son of a bitch, don't look back and hustle that cute little ass of yours back to the Enos man." That was typical Enos, he would have said that if we were lying on the beach turning an ugly pink.

Doing Jack, if you took a very broad analysis, would fall into his directive. Actually not, Enos talked about loving someone and living the rest of my life with that person, that was not going to happen with Jack. It was to be a slam-bam, thank you ma'am affair.

My position on the matter was that if it had been me that died and he was holding my hand, I would say, "Enos you deserve a happy full life. But if some other woman catches your eye, and you feel that old familiar tickle in the nether area, I hope your dick falls off and you step on it."

So, I am off to bed. It is only right that I put Boz Skaggs on for my listening pleasure. I brushed my teeth, as I leaned over the sink, I could feel the hands of my man slip under my tee shirt and touch those teacup titties He was my personal revenant.

Sunday morning came with no fanfare, I lay in bed and made the decision to skip church this morning. That made eleven hundred straight times I had made that decision. The previous day had started with an unforgettable breakfast, so this morning I wanted to have a forgettable breakfast, soft scrambled eggs and wheat toast, good coffee. All by myself. Cooking the eggs was a solid ritual for me. Crack the eggs into a small bowl, take a kitchen fork and stir while the pan heated, put a small amount of good butter in the pan and then pour in the beaten eggs, add cheese halfway through the cooking. I had some work at the library that needed to be done, but I cancelled it also. I wanted that old breakup line, alone time. I did not know where to start.

Little did she know that Ms. Katie had just said ready, set, go to the other side of this curative endeavor.

JACK'S DILEMMA

"GOD DAMN, KATIE. I know you hate that. But, God damn, are you way past nuts?"

This diatribe occurred mid breakfast. Katie seemed to have an affliction concerning a peaceable breakfast. Katie winced at Jack's explosion; she had not expected it to go down easy. Jack pushed his chair back. They were sitting in their screened in porch. The only sound came from the wind chimes. Katie did not know whether he was going to leave or throw up.

Perplexion was written in capital letters across Jack's face. He had not spoken another word since nuts. He seemed to be talking to himself while facing the floor and occasionally casting a quick glance at the pancake and bacon on his plate.

"What did you just say Jack?" Katie whispered.

I said, "Jesus hot-to-cocky Christ. I haven't said that since college, but that is the only thing that came to mind. Are you serious? Do you really want Maryellen and me to sleep together? What would that accomplish? I think your suggestion is flawed in that it presupposes that Maryellen is a very shallow person, and me too, I guess. That pisses me off. Tell me, where did this come from? I keep thinking you are nuts. Have you considered what this might do to yours and Maryellen's relationship, much less ours?"

The heat dropped from Jack's voice and he continued in a reflective fashion. "A very wise person once said something to me when we were talking about cheating on your spouse and partner. He said this, 'The best way to maintain the purity of a relationship is to never allow yourself to be in a position for cheating to occur. Weakness can occur if you get sucked into a situation that your dick won't let you walk away from, so just stay away.' You are going way past putting me in a potential discretionary dilemma. Have you thought about us? I don't think you have?" The silence of the moment was almost tactile and the distance between them grew exponentially.

Katie spoke in a low voice. "This comes from my connection with you. I realize the potential for disaster in both relationships, but my trust of your love for me transcends the fear I have of losing you to my best friend. I know, I know you are thinking that one single tryst would cause incurable damage to you and me. That is possible, if we allow it. I think this restriction of damage would be on my shoulders. I am the one that proposed it and I'm the one that stands to lose the most."

Back to Jack, "I will have to tell you, I am mad. Where in the hell do you get off putting your best friend and me, the one you love, in this cockeyed conundrum. Are you going to write a book about it? And if you did, what would exactly be the title? How about Boner Loaner, or Loaner Boner. I just don't know which would be best. Katie, I have to tell you, just your floating this scheme to us reminds me of that pseudo sexy show, Sex in the City, like having one of the girls lease out her current beau to one of the others. A happening that would be perfectly normal for one of them, but not us. There is a fissure occurring in our love, one that might not get fixed. This might seem very weird and convoluted, but I feel as if you have cheated on me. I have always considered our love a 'by invitation' only affair. The assumption being that the invitations were never even printed. Just you and me, everybody else was on the periphery. This lets someone else in the door, even if it is your best friend. It dilutes the clear intensity of our communion.

"This morning I woke up with you on my mind and knowing that you and I were good and that this day was going to be another great day in the never-ending saga of Katie and Jack. I didn't know what, whether it was our making love out in the back yard with you sitting on my lap, our eyes locked in an intensive stare with your bath robe draped around us. Maybe, our walking down a sidewalk to have a great breakfast and yes, we were holding hands during the walk.

Maybe, finding some strange foreign recipe and cooking it in the late afternoon and then throwing it away because it was horrible and eating instead a bowl of tomato soup. Now, I just don't know, I feel like a catcher who was expecting a high hard fastball and getting a slider in the dirt. If that were the case, I would go the pitcher's mound and have a conference with the hurler on the bump. I am not in the mood for that now. So, having said a lot of stuff, I am going to go away. I will be back in awhile." He slowly unfolded himself from the breakfast table without touching the food and walked out the back door.

Katie said, "Well that is two for two on rotten breakfasts."

COGITATION II

JACK WALKED TO HIS car, got in, spun the ignition and drove off. He felt like his heart had been sliced into thin pieces by a mandoline. He was astounded. He wanted to go back and talk with Katie again, but he could not. He felt as if she was on another team.

I should have known. I am going to blame it on Neal Young and soccer. Neal Young appeals to people who are a little bent, otherwise no one would listen to his stuff. As for soccer, I have believed for a long time that soccer has been the root cause of the pervasive softness in our society. That is something that I would need another complete life to explain.

It could not be possible for me to be so connected to someone right before breakfast and be blowing in the wind before I finished my coffee. I felt totally betrayed, which is ironic. My entire life I have not had one relationship when I did not cheat. It started in the second grade, I had a girlfriend named Judy and I snuck around on her with Carolyn. The pattern continued through junior high, high school, college, both young and older adulthood. If I had been a girl, I would have dutifully earned the label of two-timing bitch.

Until the day I met Katie. I made no conscious decision. I just never wanted to cheat on her. She was my best friend, my companion and there was no longer that void in my life that I tried to fill with other people. She explained it by saying I had never really been in love or had never been truly loved. Or that patented phrase, soul mates might actually be true.

Now she has suggested I jump back into a pattern that was no longer a part of my life. I felt like Katie had baptized me into mono-sex, only for me to find out she didn't really believe in it at all. Plus, the water was cold. She had not been honest with me. I am genuinely pissed. This was not a picayune pissed off. All of this miserable rambling and I still did not know what to do or who to do it with.

"Whap", all of a sudden, my death sentence joined the flood in my head. It became too much and tears made an appearance in my eyes. They did not last long, I gathered up all of my emotional pile and spit it out the window. The tears rinsed all the death and destruction off my face. As I often said, "Well, nobody died, so let's get on with it. I might have to slightly alter that to, "Well, nobody has died yet, so let's enjoy the time we have left."

About that time Dwight Yoakam came on the regular Saturday morning show, called The Bakersfield Sound. I knew what I would do if I could, I would call Dwight and talk this whole mess over with him. Anyone who could sing the heavy number of country and western hits, graduate from Ohio State University, play a part in one of the iconic movies of all time, Switchblade, carry on a conversation with Mike Nesbitt and use the word aegis in a common fashion should be the Pope. That person would have the moxie to understand and advise me in this chock full of nuts. I know I would benefit from such an encounter, but, it ain't gonna happen.

Now I am left alone to put a full nelson on this or at least part of it and bring it to heel. I keep returning to the question. What inspired this solution of sorrow by my girl Katie? Did she really think this would work? That had to be the answer. She would not put our relationship in such a precarious position. She was just wrong. She had totally misfired. Mary Ellen and I would be awkward, we were not even really good friends. Did she think that some wonderful emotional cataract would take Maryellen out of her river of sorrow? Then she would ride that cascade into a pool of water with continual waves of happiness that would drive the gray away and bring back rainbows of color. Maybe that would occur but I did not think it would happen to Maryellen just by her doing the loving feeling with me.

Then another question jumped out of the box. Was this a one-time thing or would it require repetition? What if each time only brought her out of the gray a little bit at a time? How many times would it take and how often would we have to have ingress and egress with our personals?

God, this could go on forever. What if Katie dies? Would I be obligated to continue with Mary Ellen, or would I revert back to former behavior and dump her? What to do, what to do? Damn, I hate this. Slow down, take small steps.

KASEIN GETS THE FIRST STEP

RENFROE LOOKED ACROSS THE desk at Kasein and thought to himself. What the hell. The lawyer Renfroe thought, I have to get the DNA verified. The personal Renfroe thought, I believe that girl. She reminded him of Jack, not in the looks department but her presentation of her case was Jack all over again.

"Kasein, may I call you Kasein? What exactly do you want me to do? Is it you want me to tell Jack or to arrange a meeting between the two of you? Personally, I lean towards the latter. Jack respects plain talk and confrontation."

Kasein got the response she wanted. "I would like for you to arrange a meeting between Jack and me, preferably in your office."

BACK TO JACK

I THEN HAD AN inspiration. Maryellen and I were being nominated as the guinea pigs of sex, without any thought or consideration from us. I knew what I was going to do. You know when you have a predicament and have a brainiac thought, the sun shines brighter, the leaves on the trees are greener, and the air carries a scent of vanilla. I picked my telephone up off the car seat, dialed the number of Ms. Maryellen, but quickly stabbed the cut off button before it could ring. I was not ready for conversation with anybody. I wanted a "do over" of my entire morning.

The one phrase that seemed to fit the bill was the phrase commonly used by seventy-year old men, "I am too old for this shit." That is what we say when faced with any sticky situation or decision. I then wondered, is age one of the primary planks this campaign was based on. I don't know. In an earlier time in my life, I might have acted totally in agreement with this proposition by my companion. Actually, underneath my current mask of disbelief was the true nature of Bad Jack flashing an evil grin and saying to himself." Well damn, please don't throw me in the briar patch." If that does not make sense to you, the briar patch part, ask someone who is in the seventy-year old bracket and they can tell you about Uncle Remus. I think he must have died as I haven't heard anything about him for several long times. That life of deceit is behind me now and has no place in my current situation. I sometimes wonder if I am like the murderer who gets redemption or salvation and lives the remainder of his life as a curator of propriety. Is my chastity, sans Katie, nothing more than a fleeting effort to repair my wayward soul?

I thought about that for a while and looked up to see where I was, I was driving while blind to my surroundings. I was in an area of the city that was old and carried a certain cache that made all the doctors wives want to live there. Big trees, old houses, big lots, sidewalks that were actually used in the late afternoon by couples holding hands. Tricycles and bicycles strewn across front yards. The occasional basketball goal by the road accompanied by the lonesome sound of a single teenager bouncing the ball and sometimes doing the play by play as he sank the shot to take his team to the NCAA championship.

Katie and I rode through this area lots of times when we were just riding around listening to music. We would ride and hold hands and not talk at all. I wondered how many more times we would have this blessing. It was a glorious time as if all was right with the world and we were the only ones lucky enough to know it. All of this brought it home to me, that I was living my life now as it should be, not because of repatriation or pay back for prior offenses. I was living my life because I was in the exact place, I should have been all my life. In love and in sync with a lady that I could not live without. That previous track had nothing to do with the here and now.

OK, so that problem is solved. What is next? I had noted that when Katie told me of her solution, she did not say have sex with Maryellen. She did not say make love to Maryellen. She just said she wanted me to sleep with Maryellen. Was there any significance in that or not? I thought it carried a tingle of meaning.

Katie and I talked a lot of times about what role the actual sex act played in our overall relationship. Our conclusion was that sex was a communication skill that sometimes was a healing balm. I know I said that we had only had one argument and it wasn't really that fierce. In any relationship there are times of distance or frayed feelings when we had been apart for too long or one of us said something that was misunderstood. Sex was a bridge we crossed together, to heal and recapture that exhilarating intimacy of our love. Our love was made from a recipe that only privileged people would ever know. That recipe had ingredients that were offered forth by either one of us and gladly received by the other. So, that when they combined it would make it the most delicious dish in history. We were convinced there were not many couples that were able to accomplish this.

All at once a souvenir of a night when Katie and I were having this discussion came flashing across my mind like a neon sign. Katie said to me that night. "You know Jack, I think that Enos and Mary Ellen were possessors of this charter we have. It requires protection at all times. I remember this feeling I would get when I was with them, they really were only tolerating me being there and they just as soon I leave so they could be alone with each other."

RENFROE ROOKS

THAT WAS A FIGURATIVE fork in the road for Jack, but remember he was driving, so there was also a literal fork in the road. He took the left tine and proceeded on. The neighborhood was the same and he encountered people he knew. One couple was a retired judge and his wife who was a retired teacher. They walked together every day. They just nodded to me on my way by and I returned the gesture.

I kinda knew where I was headed and let my truck continue on, until I came to a house with a big guy wielding one of those rakes designed especially for leaves in the front yard. He must have been at it for a while, there were small piles all over the yard, reminded me of my face when I was a teenager. Remember me telling you about my friend who was the titty guy? Well that was Renfroe Rooks. He and I had become business partners when we were young attorneys. Our relationship had grown over the years based on many bumping of heads and agreements to disagree. We had a mutual respect that carried us over a lot of hard times. We also shared a love of paddling a kayak. We paddled quite a bit and kayaking is conducive to talking.

Over many years of paddling together, we had a blue ton of conversations about things that the male population always pass between each other. Two boats on big bodies of water being pushed by paddles is a great place to talk about this type of thing. Basically, the only competition to the silence was the entry and exit of the paddles and wind. We talked about the usual masculine topics, football, business, the general population of assholes that passed through our office doors. And of course, our female partners, both past and present, only in very general terms. Money always reigned as the dominant piece. These topics were addressed in common conversation that we would not have minded if anyone else was aware of what had been said.

There was another level of conversation that had its own label, "Kayak Talk". This was reserved for things only between the two of us. Kayak Talk had spread its wings to anytime he and I were talking and one of us wanted to speak about one of those clandestine topics. All either one of us had to say was, "this is Kayak Talk." Both of us fully expected one of us in mid-trial to use that term during cross examination. I cannot broach this covenant between us, so I am vacating this definition and leaving it to your imagination as to what fits that bill. My impending departure was a level above Kayak talk and that is another topic.

I slowed to a stop and said "Whatcha doing?".

"What does it look like dumbass," and Renfroe never missed a stroke of raking. I got out of my truck, walked over and asked if the leaves would not disappear while he took a few minutes break.

He said. "Probably not. Why am I getting this Saturday visit? I can't loan you money, my wife doesn't really like you and I am a steward in the church which prohibits me from being a part of a lot of the things you do."

I just said "Kayak talk. I am asking you to be a backboard for me and tell me if the ball is bouncing true or if I should get off the court."

Renfroe said, "This sounds juicy and do I understand that I am to be an unbiased backboard. Not my opinion, but to adjudge if you are on the right path or not."

"Correct," was my answer. "This is a long-tailed ball of wax and I will attempt to shorten it without dilution of any part, because I know you won't sleep tonight if one leaf is left undisturbed. You have met Katie's friend Maryellen and you know that she is a widow. She was married to a gentleman by the name of Enos, I never knew him."

Renfroe interrupted, "I knew him, was involved in a few business dealings along the way. An honorable adversary."

"Well, "I said. "His demise occurred a little over a year ago. Katie and Maryellen are the very best of friends, more like a sisterhood than anything else or maybe a two-person convent with sexual privileges.

Enos has been gone for well over a year and Katie is despondent over the never-ending sorrow that Maryellen lives in, all day, every day. I am shortening this and only giving you the bullet points. Katie has come up with this idea for Mary Ellen and me to have conjugal visits. It is her gnostic opinion that our conjugation will heal the sadness. I have been mad about it ever since she told me this morning at breakfast."

As if on cue, the sun disappeared and big dark clouds took its place. Jack continued, "I think it is a crazy idea and puts not only my relationship with Katie in jeopardy, but also her sisterhood with Mary Ellen. I just don't like it. For once in my life, I am perfectly happy as I am. You know from other salacious kayak talks straightness and narrowness of my prior relationships did not exist."

Renfroe, at the most gave a half smile and said, "I think you have overloaded my ass in this dilemma, you should have taken it to the Supreme Court. Let's go in and have a cup of coffee, if Ruby will allow it."

Ruby is his wife. She was Miss Ruby to me, I knew she didn't like me, but that was okay. She always treated me as a friend of Renfroe's and my being his friend was not her decision. I liked her, but actually I think she scared me a little bit. She always maintained an attitude of rectitude, but I think that she wore a hidden bangle of mischief and could strike you like a snake if necessary.

We did get a cup of coffee and moved out to his deck. Renfroe led off, "Let's look at this proposition on its merits. If you proceed with her suggestion do you have any thoughts on it being successful, not from your standpoint, but from the standpoint of Maryellen? Would it do her any good or would you just get your dipstick smeared with self-shame? The reason I say that word shame is that as long as I have known you, this is the first time that you have wanted to play between the lines. I think that is very important to you. Without knowing any of the particulars, I think you would have a load to carry for a long time, maybe forever. Going back to my question, do you think it would work?"

Jack answered quick as a flash of light, "Cockamamie was the word I used when this proposition was first presented to me, and is still the word that is most descriptive in my mind."

Renfroe leaned back in the blue wooden deck chair and spoke in reverent tones, "I am going to make this very simple for you. Answer the question of whether it will work for Maryellen and she will gain benefit from this endeavor. If the answer is yes, then you pursue other answers to the host of questions that this begs. If the answer is no, go tell Katie that you love her and would do anything you could to make her happy, but this is not a path you could follow. It would be like walking a path along a severe mountain drop off, one misstep and it would all be over. You are not willing to put the Katie/Jack relationship at risk. You think that it will not help Mary- ellen and the damage would be irreparable to all concerned. Now, after all of this swirling around and you decide to dip your toe in the water, so to speak... I want you to understand that this does not give you license to wave your magic wand at any other wives, widows, divorcees or a vulnerable crystal closet queen, who is in conflict. I do not want to see you even give Ms. Ruby a sideways glance."

He stood up to full height and pronounced, "I have to go rake."

I got in my truck, twirled the ignition and just sat there. Sturgill Simpson flowed out of the speakers with a very appropriate song, "Life Ain't Fair and the World is Mean" ... I listened to it and spoke, "Sturgill old buddy, you are a prophet... I can see it now, Mathew, Mark, Luke and Sturgill."

The threatening skies had tucked tail and the sun had returned to its rightful place.

I realized it was approaching noon and I had not eaten anything all morning. I had one place that I guess the term -- go to place-- was applicable. I like to go there when things are very, very, good or the other side of the coin, real, real, bad. It was a skinny little place on the Main Street of town that only served hot dogs, with high quality ingredients. I would always eat at least four chili dogs all the way, a large lemonade accompanied by Lays Classic potato chips. I guess I am lucky in that whenever stress starts to dance with me, I don't want any part of alcohol... But I eat like a convict having his last meal and trying to just stretch it out just a few minutes longer.

I walked in the door, as always, the smell of cooking meat and chili sitting in a heated pot automatically lowered my stress level and made me think I had a fighting chance of coming out of this ambush alive and with only a few healable wounds. One more time it did not let me down. Should I eat my usual four or cut back now that I had thrown my hat in the ring of death. I said the hell with it and ordered four chili dogs all the way, but cut back on the potato chips. I sat with the hot dogs as company and read a newspaper that looked to be in its sixth reading.

About halfway through the second hot dog, I remembered my last visit to this establishment. There was a young lady sitting at a table across the room, she was in the company of a little girl, who looked to be about six or seven. The loop of heredity was much in evidence, both of them were beautiful. I caught them looking at me a couple of times, the little girl put her hand up to her face and giggled as only a small child can do. I wondered if they were local. I had nodded to the lady and girl on my way out the door.

The crossword puzzle was about half done, and the paper was turned to the obituary page. I wondered when I would have my place in the obits. I would not care if no one wants to pay for it. I do not want a picture of when I was about twenty years old with a Marine Corps hat tilted over to one side on my head. That always seems silly to me, and death ain't silly. The paper's former reader must have been an old person like myself or a life insurance agent.

It came to me that I had actually made a few small decisions and had gotten a very good piece of advice. How do I go about deciding if this would be beneficial to Mary Ellen and would she be happier? Could I google it? I don't think so. The only person I know who would be surfeit with knowledge of all the facts and quasi-facts in this genuine whoop de doo... has to be Mary ellen. It is not Katie's decision. It is up to the two scene stealers of this way off Broadway production, Jack and Maryellen.

Should I call or just go to her house or even worse, text her? I thought it would be fairer to both of us for our discussion to be face to face.

Her telephone number was still on my phone from my last aborted attempt to call her. She picked up on the second ring with a slight vibrato in her voice, which made me know that she had caller ID and knew I was on the other end of the line. After back and forth, hellos and how are you's, there was a deathly quiet.

I stepped out slowly with "Maryellen, would you like to talk over a cup of coffee? I honestly don't know what to think and it is my opinion that we should either have a conversation OR you can tell me, that it is not going to happen, no way no how. The first would advance towards making a joint decision, which it has to be, or you could let us both off the hook before it gets planted."

Very quietly she said, "Jack, why don't you come to my house and let me make you a cup of coffee."

"I will see you in a few minutes." In a way this scared me a little. If I had made a bet on either one of the proposals, I made to her. I would have put big money on her telling me to go home to Katie and let's forget that anything ever happened.

Her house was a white wooden house with a two-car garage in front. I noticed there were two cars in the garage, I bet one had been Enos's ride. I had been there before as a tagalong for Katie on some foray designed by the two of them to take another step to save something in the world, be it small children or big animals, can't remember. All I remember is a small kitchen and combined eating area, with a step down into a large room with big French doors. Opening to the back yard, multiple big trees and a deck. There was a boatless dock that was part of a fingerling piece of water leading into a much larger bayou. I had just lifted my hand to knock when the door opened and there she was.

Under normal circumstances we would have done one of those forty-five degree hugs which I mentioned before. Not this time. We both just stood there and tried not to stare at the other. I remembered the first time I went to Katie's house and the awkwardness that dominated our first minutes, but that awkwardness was double A baseball. This awkwardness was the major leagues.

Maryellen spoke first and it was like a hammer breaking a small glass pane. "Come in, I have some coffee waiting." We sat at the dining room table facing each other. Maryellen picked up the conversation thread. "Jack, I've had one more day to contemplate this and I feel like I have been issued an invitation to participate in a car wreck and it is just a decision on how bad I want to get hurt. What can we call it? A pyjama party, saturnalia or gala. I cannot think of anything that would fit."

I almost suggested Boner Loner, but thought better of it Being funny was not on the agenda.

She continued, "I've arrived at the conclusion that Katie has not thought this through. She is not recognizing the damage potential to both of her most important relationships. I know in my heart she in no way intended this to be hurtful to any of us... She loves both of us with all of her heart."

I interrupted with a soft "May I? I agree with everything you said, but I got some advice from a very good friend of mine. He said the bottom line is, does Maryellen think that enlisting into this possible pervasive philandering would have a positive effect on her. He did not mean a positive effect being five minutes long...To be followed by shards of guilt being hurled at both of us. He said that if you had any doubt that this would assuage your sorrow, then don't do it. If you think it might make your life happier...then the two of you should talk about it."

Maryellen made no response, but looked at me as if she was trying to get something out but was weighing it on a scale to see if she could take it back if she wanted. Would a stone have been cast that could never be caught and thrown back? I just sat there. Could not and would not say anything.

Maryellen must have made a decision, as she only said two words. "Let's talk." After that, she looked at me for a response. I still had nothing. I guess in the inner sanctum of my soul I expected and hoped she was going to say, "Jack, this is stupid and I want no part in the charade, I like you but I don't really consider this as be a possibility." But no, she wanted to discuss it. Jesus!

Just how do you discuss something like this? Do we draw up an agenda with topics of interest, or hang a board on the wall with two columns? Positives. Negatives. Can we go to Google and search for, "Discussions between a man and the best friend of his wife who are going to have sexual activities at the suggestion of his wife?" I was doing a lot of supposing in a short period of time.

Finally, Maryellen spoke. "I know you are surprised by my words, but I came to the conclusion that I could never answer the question that your friend said needs to be answered... how could anyone know? Kate talked about how our relationships were like twins and that the main reason she had finally relented to your badgering her for years, was that she was lonely. A person needs companionship and intimacy, especially as age starts to stake a claim on you. Her decision to hook up with you has proven to be a remarkable way station for both of you. Both of you reek of love, affection and happiness. At this junction of my life, I am just waiting to die. I am a ghost town. The gold mine ran out and everyone left. I am in a constant state of bereft loneliness. I can feel myself shrinking into a wedge of darkness. Is this a way for me to bring light into my life. A way to invigorate my appetite for living, a way for me to recognize and understand that Enos is gone for now. Would he want me to have an opportunity to see past the darkness? Who knows? But he is dead and I have to answer those questions for myself. A person listening to my oration would have to ask the question. Does she really mean all that falderal or does she just want to get laid?

I can at least answer half of that question, I do not want to just get laid, but a little intimacy and affection might be alright with me. Then that begs the question, and we are having a lot of questions being begged, if that is so, is Jack to be the administrator of this congress?"

Jack made a motion with both hands like he was shooting the cuffs from the sleeves of a dinner jacket, except for the fact that he had on a long-sleeved tee shirt that had a picture of an orca whale breaching on it. "I am just going to talk, things that are free frenetic thoughts in my head... First of all, you do know that I am seventy years old and the machinery in this factory is not brand new, sometimes it works and sometimes it doesn't."

Maryellen interrupted, "Speaking of machinery and the lack of reliability in your factory. Do you and Katie seek the help of tools, such as those used by Cherie?"

For the first time a little levity seemed to be legal. "Boy, you jumped right in there with that question, but you can be sure that Katie and I are sexual Luddites, we are a skin to skin couple."

Mary Ellen smiled and said, "Good, a lot of those apparati give me the willies"

I thought for just a moment and made a decision that enough had been said and mulling it over was what the next step should be.

"Maryellen, I think I should go. You don't have to walk me to the door. I think this was a good start and as we don't have a schedule, call me or I will call you and we can talk again."

Actually, we did have a schedule. We just did not know what the schedule dictated. What happens if I die in the middle of the love kingdom. It would be o.k. if I was entwined with my love bug Katie. If it was with Maryellen, would Maryellen be obligated to call Katie and say, "Hey Katie, can you come get Jack, he's dead." Does she get to put a notch on her belt. It certainly would make the local gossip headline.

DECISION BY RENFROE

RENFROE DID A SLOW stroll back out to his raking. Jack did not know but one half of his dilemma inventory. Renfroe was the carrier of the second half and it was getting heavier by the day. Renfroe came to a conclusion and dropped his rake at his feet, stuck his head inside his house and told Ruby he had to run to the office.

When he got there, he got the telephone number of Kasein, reached in his drawer, pulled out a bottle of Bullitt and poured himself a drink in his blackened coffee cup.

The phone rang a long time and was answered by Kasein who sounded like she had been running. "Kasein, I apologize for calling you on Saturday but I have decided that you and Jack should meet in my office next week. What day is good for you?

"Any afternoon but Tuesday, just let me know and remember that I cannot be there until around four o'clock."

Renfroe got caught in mid swallow, but managed to say, "I will shoot for Wednesday or Thursday. Arlene or I will call you back and finalize the details"

Renfroe leaned back in his chair and weighed his decision to set up the meeting. He came to the conclusion that it was not a decision. He had no choice. He felt much lighter as he walked down the stairs and got in his car.

BACK TO JACK

WALKING TO MY CAR I knew I had just walked out of a real door and half way understood that I may have entered a figurative door. I had no idea what might be on the other side. I picked up my phone as I waited for a red light to change. For the first time in a long damn time I felt disconnected. My relationship to Katie had been my tether, making it easy for me to float around in the air without worrying about going astray. I punched in Katie's number and waited to hear her voice. Her voice rang like a chime but with feeling "Hey, baby, where you been? I've been waiting for two or three hours."

Decisions, decisions. They are everywhere and again my relationship with Katie won out. I had spent the pre-Katie part of my life, jumping from one lily pad of lies to the next. It was second nature to me. Honesty had no place within any of my prior relationships. I often thought if they had a National Championship of Liars, I would at least get to the finals. The only time I told the truth was when the truth was beneficial to my agenda. Actually, truth was one of my best weapons, when used to establish my honesty creds with someone, it could be powerful medicine. Post Katie, I no longer had to jump those lily pads. I was a straight shooter.

Anyway, back to the question from Katie, I said, "I have been at Maryellen's house, we have been talking." She was just a few beats too slow in answering.

"Oh, did you and she discuss my proposal?" Katie's voice was hung with an attitude of an unhappy trial lawyer.

I couldn't restrain myself. "No, we discussed the upcoming city commissioner's election. We can't decide who would represent our side of town in the best manner. I know that some people don't consider this to be important stuff. But Katie, we are citizens of this town and our representation is tantamount to the ongoing success of this sleepy township in which we reside." I would have continued on but was cut short by a tart retort from Miss Katie.

No comment on my fakey Jake answer. Just "See you in a few minutes."

Everything looked the same when I pulled into the driveway. I knew I wanted back into the cocoon and to recapture my life as it had been before breakfast this morning. Between my car and the orange front door, I came to the conclusion that I was giving too much life to the Proposition. The determination that it had legs was still not clear. Before I could go forward one more step, the viability of the Proposition needed to be questioned under harsh lights. I had to start looking at this proposal like I was European. It was guilty until proven innocent. In that forty foot walk, I actually was feeling perky. Then the door opened and I still felt perky. Katie had a big smile on her face and almost knocked me down when she threw her arms around me and said, "Do you know I still love you more than anything?"

I responded with something she had said to me many times. "Me too, also."

The next six days flowed as if the world had returned to its prior axis and all was well. The Propositi was not mentioned and Katie acted like it did not exist. I think she and Maryellen talked one night on the phone and although I was not privy to the conversation, I did overhear the words "simmer and teaspoon" once or twice.

I have to admit that week was an extreme confliction for me. Women just don't look at things like men. How could the two of them talk about cooking when their relationship and the relationship between Katie and me hung like a spider's web in the rain. My conclusion was that Katie had supreme confidence that she was a visionary. Maryellen would soon be dancing and prancing just like old times. Except that Maryellen and Katie both might have dead husbands and the last big event of his life was sleeping with Maryellen.

If my demise occurred after the consummation of the Proposition, would Maryellen qualify as a Black Widow.

What if Katie wrote a book about the Proposition. I could see the following happening to us. Katie would be on a pseudo psychological speaking tour. How to Loan a Boner and Live to Tell About It. She would wear big horn-rimmed glasses, even though she didn't need them. Her agent would have advised her that this gave her creds with her audience. Would I be left at home or brought along to sit on the podium as a prop, like the box used by a magician to saw someone in half? If I stayed at home would I get phone calls from other widows? I might have to hire a screener. Was there money in it for me?

BACK TO JACK
AND KATIE

I BROUGHT MYSELF BACK down from this mental frolic, I had to remind myself that this was not funny. It was serious business. The week ended with a Friday night dinner, just Katie and me. We went to a small restaurant that overlooked a secluded cove, sat out on a deck watching small boats stream in and out of the cove, most of them carrying families to or fro. The sounds of small motors and familiar conversation backgrounded by a loop of Frank Sinatra, Dean Martin and Tony Bennett on the restaurant sound system was all there was to hear.

I am not going too far out on a limb to say we were participating in a reverie. There was no conversation between us and I wondered what thoughts were meandering around in that girl's brain cradle.

Our waiter broke the ephemeral silence with a quiet "My name is Josh and I will be taking care of you tonight." Both of our heads swung in unison from looking out at the water. Our heads went from three o'clock to nine o'clock to look at the source of the voice. We both broke into a near hysterical laugh that would not have been appropriate under any circumstances. We both looked at our waiter again. Due to the violence of our laughter, I had shot bourbon out of my nose and I thought immediately I might suffer nostril burn. Katie had choked on her pinot grigio. We both looked at our waiter again and smiled. He was probably twenty-one, but he looked like he was fourteen. We both thought it a little presumptuous that he could handle our meal tonight. The cause of our behavior was the mustache. It looked like a giant black caterpillar had crawled between his nose and lower lip. It would have been a good start on a Halloween costume.

We apologized for laughing and he stood like a statue and did not move one muscle. I ordered grouper, no sauce, a shrimp cocktail that we would share and Katie had a bowl of crab bisque. The laughing fit turned into a grand drawstring that pulled us back into our cocoon. We were back in the ballgame. Things were good again. We talked all during dinner and took a long walk along the water, holding hands the entire time, still no mention of the Proposition. That label is what I had begun to call it.

On our drive home, I thought how strange it was that one off the wall incident could repair a partially torn relationship like a tailor with a sewing machine.

We got out of the car, walked to the door with our arms locked at the elbow, entered the house and made sweet love. No hot simian affair that night. I loved her like it was to be our last time and I never wanted it to end. It was always good, but sometimes really good and it had nothing to do with the level of intensity. It was the intimacy level. Sometimes we would get lost in it and never say a word. Words were redundant… We could just lay there facing each other in our nakedness, looking at each other as our bodies closed the space between us. It would always lead to lovemaking that gathered strength like an approaching weather front… A pinnacle would be reached, fall back, and then reach another level that was like we both were reaching our hands inside the body of the other and the bodies would become one delicious sweet meld. That night was one of those nights. Afterwards we lay on our backs and I reached over to touch her face and felt the tears that had leaked out of her eyes down her cheeks. I did not know what to say, but she slowly turned on her side, reached out and pulled me to her. It was as good as life can get.

Daylight came way to soon. If someone had shown me a preview of that Saturday, I would have stayed in the bed and pantomimed death, which is probably the only acting gig I could ever really do. It now seems I will get an opportunity to play that part for real.

I got up, left Katie. She was making that noise that sounded like a low growl. This was her signature snore. I always complained, but in my heart, I knew I loved that sound. It was my sound and I did not want anyone else to ever hear it. She never jerked or flopped around in her sleep. Her sleep was a reflection of her life awake. She handled all situations with smoothness and calm which is the way she slept. I found myself sometimes getting out of bed and then just standing there as if I was listening to an ostinato that compelled me to remain in place until I felt a shower of blessedness fall on my shoulders. Then I could move.

I was the chef that morning. I wanted to be on my A game for this meal…So I went to the top of my resume. Scrambled eggs, crisp, very crisp, bacon, dry wheat toast. I knew to always start the eggs in a hot pan. I started the bacon in one pan and cooked it slowly until you could hold it by one end and it stayed horizontal. Cracked the eggs into the pre- heated pan and dropped the toast into the toaster. All of this took no more than fifteen minutes, put plates on a tray with her cup of coffee, not forgetting her favorite creamer. The butter was softened and placed in a dish beside some Katie made fig preserves.

I carried the tray carefully back to the bedroom and found her sitting up, propped against a pillow with a cat that ate the canary smile on that beautiful face. "Hey baby, what do you want to listen to this morning?"

She spoke in a sleep imbued low voice. "Annie Lenox would be great for me." I nodded consent and Annie Lenox came forth with her easily identifiable voice. We ate the breakfast slowly as if fast movements would cause the remembered remains of the previous night to run away forever.

Without speaking another word, we both knew to move very slow and it might stay just a little bit longer. I did not want to move at all, the view from the top of this mountain could not be improved on by anything. All good things start to ease away, slink away slowly really, but, we did not want to let go of the good stuff.

I went through my morning ritual with ease. Left off the shaving. Did all the rest. Re-entered the bedroom, my objet de affectione' was propped up in bed reading. "Whatcha reading? Anything good?"

She replied, "I am reading a compilation of Flannery O'Connor. Something I should have read a long time ago."

I drew myself up to what I considered haute level. "Her writing is sparse, almost like she looks at the world in black, white and gray. Didn't she die of lupus? I wonder if she went to a body farm? If so, they probably lost her due to her lack of color. She would just blend into the dirt." I continued to dress, she did not reply as I knew she considered my mini speech to be completely dumb and I was soon to be knighted into ignoramushood. I could not dispute that fact if it concerned Flannery O'Connor.

SATURDAY MORNING

I GOT IN MY truck and woke it up. It was a great truck and I considered it to be a good friend. I talked to it all the time. The aging trail provides introduction to a lot of things that were considered silly in your earlier life. Talking to yourself or inanimate objects being one of the ones that I really didn't worry about and actually kind of enjoyed it. It gave me license to comment on things that I had no knowledge of at all. I talked to closet doors, overhead lights, other drivers. I gave great, and I mean great, advice to people who seemed in conflict or consternation.

Yesterday afternoon, I passed a house with a neglected truck in the yard. The hood was up and a girl with curly, red hair was sitting on the ground leaning back against the truck with her legs asplay. She was crying and talking to herself at the same time. I asked myself, was she crying about the car not being able to run or was she was pregnant by her high school science teacher? Was her father on a three-day drunk and had her mother come out of the closet as a full-blown dyke? I could come to no conclusion, so I just said to the universe, which I expected to carry it to the red head, "Hang in there baby. Nobody died, yet."

My phone rang. It was Maryellen. It had been a week. I forced myself into blank thought and answered the phone with a forced neutral voice. "What's up?"

This generated a quick response, "I know you've eaten breakfast. I haven't. Why don't you come over and drink a cup of coffee and watch me eat a waffle and crisp bacon. We could continue our previous conversation. I am sitting at my kitchen table with a vanilla candle burning, Etta James playing in the background and wearing an unbuttoned lavender sleeping top and that's all... So, come on over."

I, being Jack, was in immediate apoplexy. I know a good sixty seconds went by that seemed hourly in time. No sounds from me. I could not breathe. What do I do now? Then I heard this weird-ass laugh come through the phone.

"You went for it didn't you? Come on over. I'm sitting here with long flannel pajama bottoms and one of Enos's old white tee shirts and my Donald Duck slippers. The lights are bright and I am listening to the morning news on the radio. You should have picked up on the fact that a sex breakfast would not have waffles as a featured item. Syrup would be messy."

I couldn't let her get away with that, so I told a little white lie of my own. "It will take a while longer to get there as I will have to sit in your drive way as the pup tent is partially up so I will have to wait until that subsides, which at my age is sometimes instantaneous." She had got me good. I had not known that side of her, but it was funny.

I felt as if I was entering from off stage to a play set. Everything was as she had described it. A slight whiff of waffle and bacon in the air and she sat cross legged at the small table in the middle of the kitchen, the only other person in the room was Aunt Jemima. She spoke first. "What are your thoughts, Sir Jack?" She picked up her plates and utensils then turned to take them to the sink.

I had never had a single salacious thought about Maryellen up until that very moment as I watched her walk across the floor. She had a knockout ass and believe it or not she had that sashay way of sliding across the floor. It is always a surprise when the male mind-wheels start to spin at an astronomical rate. Between the time she got up from the table and walked to the sink, I admired her derrière, compared her walk to Katie's, and realized although it was phantasmagorical, the scene she had drawn for me on the phone was a definite titillation.

The last thing that whizzed through my mind was that I was not far removed from the bed of my life's love. I started to speak, but Maryellen spoke first, "Just hang on. I'll be back in a minute."

I re-admired the sashay and roundness of her bottom.

Continuing my mindstream, was she a vexing vixen who had spun a vituperous vision for a vulnerable victim and had thrown that sex breakfast deal out there like chum bait? I decided not. It must have been just to lighten the mood.

She walked back into the room wearing a pair of relaxed soft gray pants and a long sleeved silky black shirt. Her low voice re-opened the conversation, "What are your thoughts on the Proposition? Do you think we should take a step towards consummation or throw any more thoughts of it into the trash bin?"

I took my time in answering this question because I thought we were at a tipping point on this decision... It could go either way. The next few minutes could decide the issue.

I replied, "I think the ball is in your court. Returning to one of our prior conversations, this whole thing hinges on whether you think it would be positive towards getting you out of sorrowland. I still think Katie, when looking back in later years will say WTF was I thinking. The problem is that the worm can has been opened and none of us will be able to forget this. It will be like permafrost. It will not go away. This is a cut that, even if it heals, will be a scar to remind us. So, having said all that, what is your verdict?"

Maryellen turned and walked away from the kitchen and into the living room and looked out the window for a few moments...While looking away from me, she started to talk. "Jack, when Enos was alive he would sometimes see a couple of older people walking down the street holding hands. He would say, there goes a love affair. Maybe not burning as bright as it had in past years but still a love affair. It was like they shared the same metier, which continued to fan the flame. Other times he would see another older couple sitting at a restaurant table, with neither player looking like they were aware of the other. Enos would say, there sits a love dirge, a relationship that has become as brittle as a potato chip. Both of them waiting for the other to die. Jack, I don't want to become brittle and I don' think that Enos would want me to wear that mantle. What I am saying is that let's go sit on the sofa, hold hands and talk."

On my way back home, I reran the film clip from our entering the room to when I walked out the door. Neither one of us had raced to meet before sitting. We did not maunder in our movements, but it definitely was not a race. We stood and faced each other and both extended a hand to the other. The joining was a gentle progression starting with touching fingers and ending with our hands in a comfortable simulation of the painting by Jan Van Eyck, the Arnolfini Marriage. I remembered this from an art class I took in college. Very strange how that returned like a gift to me. Then we sat on the sofa.

We did talk, but we might as well have been playing mumbly peg. The conversation was as stilted and out of place as a tattoo on a nun. I have trouble even remembering what we talked about. Definitely not adultery, sex habits or if either one of us had read the book Hooters Galore. The climate of the situation was just awful and was just at the point of starting to devour itself, when I, for lack of anything to say, I asked, "Do you like to dance?" Without answering she went to the music box and put on an old song by Ace, "How Long". One of those songs you remember hearing lots of times and you could sing the words to the chorus, but did not know the name of the song or who sang it.

Maryellen walked over to the sofa and reached out for my hand and said "C'mon old folks". I got up, yes folks, I could dance. We did a semblance of medium fast dancing that I had seen done on trips to Panama City in my teen years. They called it the Bop; it was one of those dances that fell into the category of a shag. It was fun and did not afford much contact between the dancers.

After the last note, she went over to the music box and Nat King Cole in his unforgettable voice sang Unforgettable. We danced kinda close and half way through the song, I felt a slight kiss on my neck as if someone had placed a circle of cool meringue there. The song continued and the end came none too soon. I dropped her hand, retracted my other hand from behind her back and left. Her front door shut without a sound. I eased into the front seat of my truck and breathed easier.

Had the die been cast? I was in a state of severe confliction as I pulled into my driveway... Oh yeah, on the way home I had noticed an older couple walking down a sidewalk, holding hands and both were laughing. Then they bent their heads together for a slight touch as if they were establishing an energy connection between them. Enos in his love affair description was mighty right.

I strolled across the green grass of our yard like a man that had just got lucky. Opened the orange door to a cacophony of California Dreaming, the Mamas and Papas. That was one of my favorite band names. The myth that followed the death of Mama Cass was untrue. She did not die from choking on a ham sandwich... She just had an ordinary old fat girls heart attack.

I emerged from my reverb dream to a voice that asked, "Where you been lover boy?" trying her best to imitate Sylvia of Mickey and Sylvia.

Sticking to my plan of open architecture like duct tape, "I have been to Maryellen's."

Katie had been bending over the sink dancing to the music, I caught an ever so slight hiccup in the butt wiggle and she turned with hands on her hips and said, "Well, look at you. Let's go out to lunch."

"It's only 10:30".

"Good", she answered, "we will beat the crowd." So, we walked out the door without further discussion.

LUNCH WITH
THE ROOKS

IN THE TRUCK, WE began the eternal couple food forum debate... Where to eat. We both hated chains and especially the ones, where upon your entrance, someone would cry out, Welcome to Charley's or whatever. You wanna go to the beach, nope too many tourists with new white tennis shoes on their feet. It seems like it is mandatory for someone who comes to the beach. You have to have brand new white tennis shoes, the white sets off the pink of their sun burned legs.

Katie suggested, "Let's go to Susie's. You can get oysters, good gumbo, plain fried or grilled grouper without some goopy sauce, and an unusual offering was the best hamburger steak you will ever have." Susie's was one of the few restaurants in our town that did not fall into the category of tourist trough. It had asmall dining room with an oyster bar to one side. Authentic photos of Panama City in the old days were hung all over the walls. We walked in and sitting at a nearby four top table was Miss Ruby and Renfroe, we immediately were summoned over and not asked but assumed that we knew to sit down and join them.

Renfroe spoke first, "Well how is the royal couple this early morning?"

Katie answered quickly, "Stunningly good. No health issues. Sex is passable and it isn't raining.

Ruby immediately entered the arena, "Before I forget to ask, I just went by the library to drop off my borrowed books and Maryellen wasn't there. I asked and was told that she was supposed to be in the morning, but she called and said she would be a couple of hours late. She had a personal issue to resolve. Is she okay?"

Again, that slight hiccup in her actions before Katie answered, "As far as I know she's fine, I haven't talked with her in a couple of days. She might have some type of twenty-four hour virus. I will give her a call."

It was like a faint rain descended over the table.

I caught a quick glance from Renfroe, that said plainly, uh oh. He had an innate ability to recognize danger.

Katie rose to the occasion and asked Ruby if she was doing any jewelry construction, as they had done some of that in the past.

I felt comfortable in the fact that Renfroe had not violated the Kayak Code with Ruby. If he had, Ruby would not have said anything about Maryellen at all. Renfroe might have asked about Maryellen just to have a little fun and get to watch me squirm.

I smartly kept my mouth shut tight, giving the appearance that I was totally focused on my roasted oysters. I could see no benefit in my getting involved in this vocal miasma.

All during the meal I would catch Renfroe shaking his head as if he was having an internal discussion, debating whether to say anything or not. I know he was dying to spread kerosene on the fire, like saying, "Jack have you seen Maryellen lately? I am curious about how she so cavalierly did not show up for work the morning." He knew he clutched my boys in his hand and could cause death and destruction with a vigorous squeeze. But he kept a tight rein on his mouth and I lived to play another day. The meal meandered on to an easy death.

As we walked to the cashier station, Renfroe sidled up to Jack and said,' "Jack can you come by the office Wednesday around 4:15 or so. I have something that I need your opinion on and I want to have a little time for us to discuss it."

"Sure, no problem. I will see you then."

Little did I know that a life changing event lay in wait for me at that meeting.

Goodbyes were exchanged with the only blemish being Ruby asking Katie to tell Maryellen she had asked about her. A common practice amongst us Southern folk.

The ride home was quiet, which was unusual. I noticed this older couple walking down the sidewalk. They looked straight ahead, their appearance was stonelike and their being consanguineous was a real possibility. They could have had small neon signs above their heads that said, "No Love on Board" or wore tee shirts that said "I'm with Stupid." Definitely a love dirge. I wondered if this was an omen for the remainder of what I shall call "Disparate Saturday".

The afternoon drifted along like a weak stream. Katie retreated into our bed and I assumed was soon captured by a nap. I sat on the sofa, the only thing moving was my right hand as I used the TV remote like a professor's pointer. None of the shows offered me any respite from my discombobulation. I continued to track up the guide and back down again. Then I saw it. The Rolling Stones concert in Havana, always a great opportunity as they non-compromised showmen.

Ronnie Woods, the ultimate teenager who had all the clothes, but just wasn't as cool as the other kids. Keith Richards, a man who looked like he had participated in at least one hundred years of a degenerate life, but he still loved to play that guitar. Mick Jagger, the one who was off in all directions but was still the consummate showman. Charlie Watts, sitting with a straight back and looking like an ancient bird amongst his drum kit.

I watched it for about two hours, but with only about half of that with my eyes open. At that point in my life, sometimes I just woke up after sliding into an unplanned siesta. The thought crossed my mind that there might be a nap one Saturday afternoon that would not end.

Upon waking, my mind became a pinball bouncing from one flipper to the next and just as I approached some sort of resolution, it would go TILT. It pissed me off that Katie had dispatched me into this continuum. At this moment, I loved Katie as much as I ever had. Since the first second of being aware that she was the provider of an existence that I had never known before. I actually never even knew existed. I had always thought relationships between people were doomed to rot and extinction. There was always a time limit imposed on love, to be followed by a humdrum period and then destruction.

I had not checked but if I had, I would know that Katie was tossing around in the bed, napping was not on the agenda. She was having a conversation with herself, she felt like she was having a one person wrestling match.

Katie was afraid. Afraid that the relationship with Jack was becoming discolored. A more accurate description was the term "foxed", the color of old books with brown spots. Ironically, she had learned that word from Maryellen. Her buddy, Maryellen, the carrier of the sorrow disease which Katie thought she could cure by making Jack her concubine.

The solo conversation went something like this. "Although I know that status is supposed to be of the female gender. I tried to put a harness on my aerial thoughts, I did not know anything other than Jack had been to her house twice. I really shouldn't count the first one as it was immediately after I shared the proposal with Jack and he was in mental disarray when he left the breakfast.

"When I came up with the idea, I felt good about it, as I had complete trust in the two of them. I did have a firm belief that Jack would only be used as a mnemonic of what affection and love had been with Enos. My feeling about the whole thing was beginning to curdle like old milk."

I needed to talk about this." I got up and went into the living room. "Jack" I said, "Is it ok if I went over to Cherie's house?"

"Sure, don't stay too long."

Katie could not help it. "How was your visit with Maryellen?"

He seemed to hesitate. His thoughts were like scattered marbles and he needed a moment to gather them together. "Well, we talked about stuff, can't remember anything in particular. Oh yeah, she was finishing breakfast and you won't believe what she had on. Flannel pajama bottoms and a soft well-worn white tee shirt. We talked and she told me some things about Enos. I wish I had known him. He seems to have dug a deep trench and poured a strong foundation in looking at life and love. Did Maryellen ever tell you about love affairs and love dirges. I also discovered she has a full grown sense of humor. Then we danced."

Katie in an incredulous tone said, "You danced at 8:30 in the morning? What else did Fred Astaire and Ginger Rogers do this a.m. Slow dancing or fast dancing?"

Jack in an easy manner said "Actually it was 9:15. Both. We danced slow and fast. She kissed me on the neck." Jack wrapped that last part in Saran Wrap, so that Katie could see it all. He had not withheld evidence.

Katie smiled as if she was satisfied that she was a master planner seeing proof that her plan was good. She casually said over her shoulder, "See you in a little while." She walked out the door and said one word, "Shit."

ADVISE AND CONSENT FOR KATIE

CHERIE'S HOUSE WAS, AS always, spotless and nothing was out of place. Katie had always been amazed because the house did not seem to fit its owner. The decor was modern, as if it was owned by one of those tall skinny women in the society section of the New York Times. It was tastefully decorated by all standards, no matter where you looked, artisan pottery and glass statuettes by Hans Frabel were present in multiple places. Her dinner ware was understated and looked like it should never be scratched by a fork. Original paintings hung from walls covered with paper that had to have been hand styled. A certain perfumery of the house was something I had never encountered in my life. I just knew that the word smell was insufficient and wrong. All of this spoke nothing of the owner.

"Cherie, I am always flabberfaced every time I walk in your house. You must have made a hell of a lot of socks in your younger days."

She casually answered as if she had answered that question many times before. "Well, I will just say, I made a hell of a lot of somethings or someone's, and it had nothing to do with socks."

We leaped over the usual hello, and how are you and landed in the sand pit of my dilemma. "Cherie, what have I done? I think I have jumped upon the shark. Jack came home from being with her this morning. He said they danced and she kissed him on the neck and she had a good sense of humor. Now that's going a little bit too far. I imagined they would conjoin but it shouldn't go so far as for them to have fun. I just don't like the way this is headed."

Cherie looked like she was deep in laugh repression mode. She had never seen Ms. Smooth Katie let go of the controls. "Miss Katie, you may have loosed the hound lady. Maryellen might have been growing a nice set of horns during the past year and decided to take receipt of the package delivered to her by her best friend. She might call it, 'Your best friend's lover with benefits.' As for having fun, you did not exactly sanction an event that evokes sadness. Think about it. She can do this without repercussions and without fear of becoming involved. She knows that Jack loves you like life itself. So, she might use Jack as an entry vehicle back into life. Maryellen is not your typical old blue haired mademoiselle. She had an active loving fulfillment of her sexual appetite and that appetite might be calling for sustenance. Kinda like a bear coming out of hibernation who doesn't really care if she eats her good friend's fresh kill. Having said all that, remember what Jack always says in bad times: Did anybody die? Well good, let's get on with it. Katie, you have the dynamite to blow this up. Just tell them you were wrong and you don't want it to continue. Why don't you go and talk with Maryellen?"

Katie got up, walked across the floor, looked over her shoulder and gave a slight wave of her hand, sashayed out and closed the door behind her and said one word. "Shit."

Katie sat in the still quiet car and immediately leapt into deep conversation with herself. Well, I might as well go for the trifecta, the decision to go to Maryellen's house slid out of my head like a kid on a sliding board. Guess what? No one's home. I bet she went to the library... Post tryst. This might be one of those omens that says I shouldn't talk with Maryellen. I called upon myself to make a good decision. Not one dripping with emotion, but one that would stand the test of time.

Maryellen had been my friend for many years. We had been through lots of bad times. A miscarriage, a stalker, being broke both financially and heartly, Enos dying and her eternal sorrow. All of these things we had plowed on with the determination of two oxen. We plowed until the bad times folded like a night blooming cereus in the morning light. We were a formidable team. A person is a fortunate soul to have one friend like that in their entire life. I felt I had two, Jack and Maryellen. It wasn't like I made a choice to go in and see Maryellen. I had no choice. I had to see Maryellen.

She was seated at her desk, totally absorbed in some paper she was reading. That was good. Sometimes when Jack and I made love I would go into what I called an orgasmic fog. I would walk around, sit on the couch and look out a window or sing softly to myself. Anything that did not require me to mesh the mental gears. So, if Maryellen could concentrate on some official library business, that might be a good inkling that it was only a chaste kiss, not the kickoff of a sexual super bowl.

"Hey baby," I said. Whatcha doing?"

Maryellen's head snapped up with authority. After all she was the head book minder. "I am reading an article on toe fungus. You remember that time a long time ago we had a conversation about that permanent evil. It seems that probiotics might be something more than a panacea for that particular affliction. Enos had it. Does Jack?"

Katie immediately applied that info into the data bank. If Maryellen didn't know if Jack had the affliction, then it follows that she has not seen his toes. But then, what if they had SOS sex, or the lights were off and shades drawn tight? Katie said to herself, put yourself in irons, you are going way too fast. "No, Jack has girly toes... No fungi for my man." Stone silence and it was genuine stone silence. She decided to pull out her hammer and chip off a big chunk.

"I understand you and Jack got together this morning. Early morning dancing will certainly get the blood flow going."

Maryellen raised her eyes from the fungus article and said very slowly, like each word was being inspected for flaws. "Katie, was that a 'no sweat, no problem, I am good with it' voice or was that a 'what the hell' voice? Now remember, you birthed this rendition of psychological protocol and had all sorts of reasons why it might work and that you were good with it. I think you used the term seldom as a time interval that we could sleep together. Well, we are well within those papier mache boundaries... So, if you want to recant your proposal, just say so. But, until you decide to flip flop like a fish on a dock, Jack and I are being very careful in our concubinous efforts... Which is it? Thumbs up or Thumbs down? We can go either way, and I love you like I always have and this whole mess will disappear like a road sign out the rearview mirror."

Now that the ocean liner in the room had set sail, Katie had the look of flummoxia. She seemed to be paralyzed, as if posing for a sculpture. The solitary audience watched Katie as she did that thing that women do before going out. She looked at the front of her shirt, then looked as if she was looking in a mirror at the back to make sure it hung just right. Then she spoke in a voice that could only be described as gut speaking.

"I don't know what to say. My commitment to easing your sorrow is still paramount to my path. I thought I was capable of doing just about anything to restring your life and return you to me fully in tune. In retrospect, selfishness was part of this hunger to have you repaired so that we could be Katie and Maryellen again.

"I am still on board that the idea could work and I am cognizant of the fact that I might lose a little piece of my life. I have tried to imagine what I would say to Jack if he came home and I could tell he had made love to you. I'm not saying that it would not be hurtful, but I am not anticipating a permanent scar." Her awkward pause hung in the air like a small bird learning to fly.

Maryellen spoke like she had her hand on a Bible. "What are you saying? Give me a go/no go or do you want an opine from me?"

Katie again assumed the pose and answered, "Yes. What do you think?"

Maryellen, remained in her chair, minus her usual business lady attitude, but dead calm. "When you ladled this hot idea of yours out to me, I was astounded and I completely rejected it on every level, but as you know I still converse with Enos. He continues to take the position that I might have mergers with others after he has flown but with the caveat that upon my opening the death door, we join forces again, in whatever zone that surrounds us. After retrieving a lot of reminiscence from the compost pile of my existence, I have come to the conclusion that a little skin might help me crawl out from under the bed and face life again with some vigor."

Maryellen rose from her chair and looked Katie straight in the face. "So, my answer is, if you can handle this thermo nuclear potato, I am willing to proceed. Since I am caveating around, I will give mine to you. The one event that would permanently and I am talking 'forever' here, cause damage to our relationship is if you lower your stop sign here to let things pass through and things do pass through. You know what I am talking about. Then, at that time you blow your whistle, throw a flag and call penalties on Maryellen and Jack. You and I, and probably you and Jack would have the internals ripped out of our bindings. We would be done. Now, give me a hug and get on out of here. I have things to do."

Kate did a minor pirouette and walked down the hall. Maryellen thought she heard Katie say," Shit."

Maryellen watched her sashay down the hall and wondered what was going through that minefield of a mind. I know what she says, but sometimes saying something prior to being actually presented with the detritus of an event is totally askew with the resultant true actions of the sayer.

It had always been fascinating to Maryellen the different perceptions of the sexual enterprise. Some people treat it as they would a blue sapphire diamond the size of your palm, it is the epitome of an emotional and physical encounter. Others treat sex as they would an old shoe. Equivalent to a kiss on the hand and certainly nothing about which you would blow your brains out.

Maryellen always thought of Katie as a midstreamer. Sex was important but it definitely not something to lose a lot of sleep over. I just wondered how she would react when Jack came home one day and she knew he and I had done the deed. He would not have to say anything. She knew Jack. If he walked in the door, within thirty seconds she would know. He might as well have hung a neon light around his neck that looked like a backbar beer sign that said, 'We Did It.' This would be her opportunity to have a "come apart" moment. The loco locus, or she could casually say "I don't feel like cooking. Why don't we go out to eat? I have been watching this football game and why does one team get six downs and the other only got four." At this point, it could either be an Indian war dance or a Russian ballet. I don't have to worry about that now. I think I will go home, eat a peanut butter and banana sandwich and sing a few Elvis songs.

JACK AND KATIE BEACHING

JACK SAT ON THE sofa fighting the failure of his eyelids to stay in the open position Not an uncommon occurrence on a Saturday afternoon for him. Two teams were playing football and he had no idea who they were, just red/black against blue/gold.

A thought scrambled across his mind. What in hell did Renfroe want to talk about at the meeting in his office. Was it a per usual meeting where he just wanted me to confirm a decision he had already made on a legal matter. Probably so. You never know about him, it could be a health situation, hopefully it would not be about him or Ruby. Oh well, I will soon find out.

Then the door opened and Katie walked through the door with just a little too much energy. Just her stride told him that all was not well in Katieville. She gave him a brief glance and he wisely let his eyelids dictate a faux nap. She went into the kitchen and he heard something hit the countertop with more than a little force. The harsh stride continued into the bedroom and shoes were launched into the closet with small swift kicks. He thought he could hear her talking to herself but could not make out the words. He continued to do his best Rip Van Winkle. He could feel her presence like black clouds scudding across the sky and you knew it was going to rain. But no. She sat down next to him at the end of the sofa and softly extended her legs and ran her scrumptious toes lightly down his thigh. His hopes immediately leapt to "hot damn" levels.

She softly said, "Jack, do you love me?"

In that short time, Jack overcame his self -induced narcolepsy and was fully awake. "Baby, I love you like powdered sugar loves French toast."

"What the hell does that mean, lover boy," her voice on the 'lover boy' dipped down into luscious territory? "Why don't you get your lazy ass up and let's go down the beach and drink and eat into the sunset. You have to answer my question before you arise. Just what the hell does love have to do with powdered sugar and French toast?"

"Think about it", he said. "Powdered sugar has one major function in life, to spread itself upon warm French toast. I am the powdered sugar and you are the delectable crisp on the outside, soft on the inside French toast. Simple descriptive phrase that makes all the sense in the world to this po boy."

"Where we going? Do I dress up, dress down, come just as I am without one plea?"

The Baptist in Jack snuck out from behind the pew.

She placed her forefinger on the side of her nose and said "Let's get in my Jeep and ride with a cold beer in our hands. Just head west until we see where we should be."

The next thing I knew, I was riding shotgun in a white jeep with the top down and ZZ Top chasing us down the road with "Got Me Under Pressure". It was October and there was a slight tingle of chill announcing the coming approach of winter. The fall was always the best time of the year. Not to cold, not to hot, sunsets that were stunning and painted in horizontal panels of richness and glory.

Katie was my pilot. She always drove with abandon and if she tucked the intermingled gray strands of hair under her hat, she closely resembled an eighteen-year old girl taking her grandfather out for a ride. Nothing was said for a while. We just rode and sipped our beer like secret agents. I had a feeling I knew where she was heading. There was a place we went to at least once or twice a year. It was a go to place for us. Beachey Keen. It was owned by a guy we had come to know over the years. Alisondro Keen. He was the offspring of a small, red headed freckled face hombre from Nebraska and a rotund senorita from somewhere in Mexico. It was a great place to sit, drink and watch the sunset. You walked through a small entryway, which opened into a large room with a horseshoe shaped bar festooned with sombreros and cowbells. The clientele was always the same. Gray hair, mottled skin, wrinkled mouths, sitting in semi crouch while casually smoking cigarettes. Conversations were low and you always felt you were entering into a members only affair. Everyone knew everyone. We selected a loveseat kind of thing where we could watch the sun give it up. On this type of occasion, we always ordered a drink we say we invented, but probably didn't… Equal parts of Mt. Gay rum and water, add ice and a good squeeze of lime juice. A very clean taste.

We had not talked at all on the ride out and continued our silence until we had broken the seal on our cocktails. I turned to her and said, "How was your day?"

At the same time, she said, "I went to Maryellen's." It was a synchronicity that failed. It only increased the uneasiness that hung in the air like an icicle that would not melt. I recovered enough to say, "You go ahead," and so she did.

"I went to Maryellen's. I also went to Cherie's."

Before I could break in with a "You've been a busy girl."

She continued, "Both gave me the same present just wrapped in different paper. They said, while pointing at me, you have birthed a conundrum child and tossed us all into a quandary quarry. The final results could beget more fireworks than the night of the Star Spangled Banner's birth. They said our relationship might succumb to constant strain and even strangulation, figurative not literal. Maryellen and I might not speak again. But and there is a real but, they both agree that I could step in and wave the red flag and stop all of this, dead in its tracks. I need another drink and what do you think?"

Jack did not hesitate with his answer as he held up his hand with two fingers motioning to the waiter.

"I think I want to get in a time capsule and go back at least three weeks, back to when we had clear blue skies over us and sunsets competed with sunrises in a beauty contest every day. I want to know that you and I remain above the fray of other lesser beings. That Neil Young was the only disputable rock in our lives. If Maryellen is in a ditch of sorrow and you think sex might mitigate her pain, bake her some cookies in the shape of a jumbo penis or buy her one of those sex toys that goes in and out, enlarges, warms up, vibrates, rotates and plays a Blues Traveler harmonica piece all at once. I am very fond of Maryellen, but she is a big girl and grief can take a long time to let go. I am in love with you in a manner that I did not think existed, but love can let go. Someone or something can reach down and peel your fingers off the bar one at a time until you fall and poof it is gone. So, my answer is this, I don't want to take the chance on doing one smidgen of damage to Jack and Katie." A person listening to our conversation would adjudge me to have said the same thing that Cherie and Maryellen said, but again, wrapped in different paper."

Fresh drinks arrived and we both sat and stared at the sunset.

Katie slithered over next to me like a seductive snake, rested her head on my shoulder and held my hand. We had always had a special way of holding hands. She would curl her hand into a little fist and I would wrap my hands around it She said that always made her feel comfort and safety against everything. I liked it and considered it a vote of confidence that I would never do anything to hurt her. Somehow in moments of reflection, I always went back to that day when I told her that very thing. Funny how small things become big things in a relationship and acquire relevance to the reverence of our love. I don't think I can accept death. It will have to go somewhere else. I cannot go at this time.

She spoke in a soft whisper that only I could have heard, "Baby, let's go home, put on some good music, get in the bed and do a fine rendition of Nekkid Dancin. I need to feel your warmth upon my soul." Soon after that the Jeep was cranked and we headed to the house. Beth Hart trailed us with 'I'd Rather go Blind.'

Sunday morning came and went, Monday morning came and went, and so on until it was Wednesday afternoon.

THE JACK AND KASEIN MEETING

JACK WAS RUNNING A little late as he drove into the parking area of Renfroe's office. The only cars present were Renfroe's truck and one of those small SUV vehicles that ran on air. Jack wondered whose car that was. Renfroe's office was a two-story box with lots of glass, stone and heavy doors. Big oak trees surrounded the building like sentinels on guard. Jack entered the building and was greeted by a host of silence. No one was in the lower level and he climbed the stairs that led to Renfroe's office. He had traveled these stairs countless times over the years of his practice with Renfroe, never with the trepidation that had suddenly taken root in his soul. Slivers of fantods ran through his body like small fish. He did not know that Renfroe had sent everyone home. Renfroe wanted this meeting to be a private affair. If an emotional outburst occurred, he wanted it to be nobody's business.

The door to Renfroe's office was closed, which was unusual at this time of day. Jack gave it a quiet knock. The knock was followed by a familiar voice, "Come on in."

Jack entered the room and immediately knew that this meeting was not going to be what he had expected. One of the two big leather chairs that faced Renfroe contained a female. He could not see her face as she had not turned when he entered. Renfroe gestured with his left hand for Jack to be seated in the other chair. Jack thought, *he looks like a maître d seating someone at a restaurant, not like a former law partner and friend, who would have said, "Sit your ass down, do you want a drink?"*

Jack assumed the countenance of a client and sat down.

Renfroe leapt into the awkward silence and his voice, which normally was a functional growl, came out more like a squeezed bleat. "Jack, I am going to offer my apology prior to anything else. I have not been clear to you on this meeting. The purpose of this meeting is for me to introduce you to this young lady across from you. Her name is Kasein Russell, she lives a short distance from Panama City and has a daughter, six years old who goes by the name of Kalia."

Until that moment, Jack had continued to look straight at Renfroe. He was not confused to this point, but it was right around the corner. He slowly swung his head to face Kasein and you could tell something clicked. "I saw you in the hotdog stand about a month ago. You were with your daughter."

Kasein, looked deep into Jack's face and very softly said four words. "She is your granddaughter."

Jack sat back in his chair and looked like he was adding up numbers in his head. No one said anything. The only sound was the ticking of the grandfather clock in the corner of the room. In a voice that could not be construed as a "whoopee" voice, Jack said, "Am I to assume that you are a prior unknown *Love Child*?"

Renfroe thought to himself. *This is not good, that is Jack's courtroom voice.*

"I have often wondered if many years ago I set this surprise in motion. Until tonight I thought I had passed the time in my life when I might discover that I was a father. I really don't know what to say." The tone of his voice was without life.

Renfroe knew he had to rescue this meeting as it was heading for destruction. "Jack, I apologize again for my setting this meeting. I did not know how else to make you aware of your daughter and granddaughter. Kasein came to see me last week and in essence hired me as her attorney. Under most circumstances, I would not have accepted this assignment. She did not have this knowledge until about a year ago. One afternoon her mother called her and asked her to come for a visit. Her mother was in the midst of a battle with death, courtesy of cancer. During this meeting, she informed Kasein of your parentage. Kasein has no desire to interrupt your life in any way, especially financially. This meeting was not just based on her mother's revelation. That occurrence during your lunch in the hot dog stand was not a chance meeting. After you left, she picked up your drinking cup and had the DNA test done This solidified the fact that you are her father. Her goal in this is for you to have a relationship with her daughter. Kasein is a teacher and has a good life. She was once married, but it was only in place long enough for her child to become a part of her life. "Kasein, did I leave anything out that you think is relevant?"

"Yes, there is one other thing that is lurking out there like an unseen spirit. Jack, after my mother died, I decided I needed to have a physical examfrom stem to stern. Cancer carries the ability of heredity and I have a beautiful child that I did not want to leave in this world alone. I never intended to contact you until my mom died and all of this came to me like thunderhead clouds in a late August afternoon.

Jack, almost smiled, but it was not a happy smile. It was a smile cup filled with irony. He looked at her and spoke, this time with a cushioned baritone. "I am familiar with that situation. I would like to know your mother's name and the circumstances of conception. That had to be at least thirty years ago and my memory is now etched with forgotten episodes." Jack knew this came our wrong, but Kasein was not fazed one bit.

"Her name was Linda Russell. She had an early thirties crush on you and one of her friends called you up and asked you to assume the position of birthday present for her. I often wondered what would have been the outcome if you had said no. But, you didn't. The birthday night grew into a two week or so torrid affair."

Jack spoke with recognition in his voice, the stentorian traces were gone, "Now, I do remember. You are correct on the time, two weeks or so, we called it 'sex, alcohol and rock and roll. I think we wore each other out, we knew when it was time to walk away. Probably the most peaceful parting of my entire life. During the past several years, I have often thought of her. You wear a strong resemblance to your mother."

Renfroe had been prepared for outbursts, stomping out the door, screaming accusations, but not for this calm collected reaction from

Jack. Maybe he will go out in the parking lot and do a whirling dervish dance, but so far, NOTHING. Then the real reason poked its head out. It was all about Katie.

"Kasein, I have a relationship with a lady name Katie and she is the most important thing in my life. I don't know where we should go with this at this point, but I am going to leave now. I have to talk with Katie. Can I call you next week? Renfroe, you have her contact info?" Both of them nodded, yes.

He stood up and turned to Kasein. It was easy to see he did not know how to end this confrontation. He stuck out his hand in an awkward fashion, like he did not know whether to leave his hand out there or to stick it in his pocket. Kasein, did not reach out to his hand. She said very softly, "Could we have a short hug to end this introduction." And they did.

Jack thought to himself as he eased into the driver's seat, here goes another one of those rides that I won't remember until I get there. For once music was not a necessary backdrop. His mind did an exercise that reminded him of a word he read in some book somewhere. Debouchment, something that starts in a narrow space, that being he and Kasein in Renfroe's office, and then expands into a wide open area, that being the granddaughter, Kalia and Katie. His becoming a father and grandfather, his impending life end, and more stuff than he chose to forget at the moment. And then he was in his driveway.

He walked in his front door and there she was, like she knew he had news to tell. Jack could not speak. He could only look at her.

Sometimes after a relationship enters the maturation process, the two involved lose their enthusiasm for their partner, but this was not the case with Jack and Katie. Jack looked at her like it was the first time. Her beauty was still exciting to him. The face was perfectly arranged as if an artist had been given discretion on each part and its placement. Her hair was still a startling feature, it flowed in torrents in all directions with slight curls here and there.

Jack lifted his hands to cradle her face, gave her a quick kiss and said, "Baby, we need to talk." Still holding her hands. They walked to the couch.

"I just left a meeting at Renfroe's office. I thought it was a meeting for Renfroe to pick my brain about some case he was involved in, he has done that several times in the past. It was not that type of meeting. I wish I could think of a way to give you this news, but."

Katie interrupted, "Spit it out, Jack, quit stalling."

"Renfroe introduced me to a lady, Kasein Russell. She is my daughter. I had no knowledge of her prior to that moment. She apparently did not know I was her father until about a year ago. Remember my telling you about the time I was requested as a birthday present for someone I did not know. Well, I was not the only present she got for her birthday. She never contacted me. One other thing, Kasein has a daughter."

Katie just sat there with no reaction at all. Jack did not know what to do.

Slowly Katie raised her head and looked Jack straight in the eye. "We have to get married tomorrow. I cannot be a grandmother without being married."

THE NEXT DAY.

RENFROE CALLED EARLY THE next morning. "Jack, how are you? I know I have apologized at least twice already, but, again, I am sorry for the unexpected splash made in your life last night."

Jack responded, "I don't know if there is a good way to break that news to anyone."

Renfroe in a hesitant fashion, "I know this is not good time, but if I need you, could you come to my house on Saturday morning and help me with a project I am working on?"

"Only if you are not going to introduce me to another love child. One is quite enough at this point in my life."

Jack could hear Renfroe give a sigh of relief over the phone. "You have my solemn promise. What are you doing late this afternoon, I would like to buy you a drink?"

In a very ordinary voice, Jack replied, "I can't. I am getting married this afternoon and you can't either because you are going to tell Arlene to cancel any appointments you might have. You are marrying Katie and me at three o'clock today in your office. I will see you then. Got to go."

Jack had a big smile on his face, he had heard the beginnings of sputtering as he hung up the phone. Serves him right.

I was glad to work with Renfroe on Saturday. I did not want to be unoccupied and have to make a decision that included Maryellen. I had not talked with her all week.

Katie took the day off. She owned a boutique out at the beach. She was its best advertisement. We agreed to meet at Renfroe's office and do the deed. I know we both were excited but were trying to be cool about the whole thing. I left and drove over to Seaside and bought her a ring.

And we got married that afternoon.

Renfroe called Friday night early and confirmed if I would come to his house Saturday morning and help him with a project he was working on. I thought this was a little awkward, but nothing stood in the way of Renfroe's projects.

MARYELLEN
THREE TIMES

I KNEW WHAT I would be doing when I got to Renfroe's. It would involve carrying, holding heavy stuff, or unloading something. He was very aware of my lack of any skill at anything to do with construction type activity. This fact dictated my participation to be limited to what is called common labor. He was already sweating despite the moderate temps and was walking across his yard carrying a monstrous toolbox. "I see you are already getting my tools ready, what will I be doing today, leveling, mitering, nailing, screwing stuff together, cutting angles. What will it be?"

Without slowing a step, he said, "Jack, mitering and cutting angles are pretty close to being the same thing. Just remember this, bourbon and water always seeks its own level. So, you will be carrying stuff to me and I will be doing the important magical tricks.

"There will be mid-morning snacks and plenty to drink. Oh yes, there will be good conversation and we might even speak of your on-going commotion at hand. Before we get started, bring me up to date on the latest episodes involving Jack, his new uncommon wife and her best friend."

"My first two days of marriage have been a resounding success. Yesterday, I called Kasein and asked if we could drive over and Katie could meet Kasein and Kalia. We drove over in the afternoon. Katie was wonderful, she did that duck to water thing on being a grandmother. She and Kasein at first were like each was walking around with a grenade in their hand, but as you know, Katie can be persuasive when she wants something. I think she wants this to be a good thing. It did not take long before they were talking about dresses, recipes and facials. As for Kalia, it was like they had known each other from birth. Katie and Kalia seemed to share a special common ground that occurs sometimes between grand people. Renfroe, I am a lucky man."

Renfroe would not let him off the hook. "C'mon what happens next? Can I tell Ruby? More importantly, does Maryellen know?"

Jack, who seemed to be enjoying himself, said. "You are the sole proprietor of this *breaking news*. I am hiring you as my attorney right now, here is five dollars. You cannot violate client/attorney privilege by telling one soul, to include Ruby. I would like to be a spectre so that I could watch you practice escamotage, as you talk with Ruby. I have always been a little suspicious as to your silence when it comes to Ruby. You would barter anything to obtain sexual entry into Ms. Ruby's Garden.

"Kasein and Kalia are coming to my house on Sunday for dinner."

I had a fine week sans Maryellen and really did not want another tranche to come up for air today, but Renfroe would not be deterred. "C'mon, this is my male soap opera, I need a new fantasy. The one I've been using is as worn as a year-old comic book. Give me a ducat into the Intimacy Theater of which you are the producer, star and ticket taker. I need some fresh material. I caught Ruby trimming her nails with her arms around my back the other night right at the peak of my invectus deflecti."

I, being a living Jack, could not let this dead horse get beaten any longer. "Hold it. There is no such thing as invectus deflecti and don't say there is because I have conducted an extensive survey of all the synonyms of fucking and invectus deflecti is not one of them."

"Damn, you caught me," Renfroe said with just a tinge of chagrin, "Ruby doesn't know that. She just thinks I am a sophisticated man of the world. C'mon give me just a tiny taste of it."

I surrendered. "There is not much to tell. We saw you at lunch shortly after I left Maryellen's house. It has only progressed to slow dancing and a kiss on the neck. In addition, lots of talking."

"Damn, that's it? Well hell, we might as well work".

Two hours later, he had fixed a door frame that was out of square. It looked okay to me, but he could not stand to just read a book on Saturday morning. He always had these perpetual projects. Anyway, I left.

The phone rang as I was getting in the truck, it was Maryellen. I answered, before I could speak. She said, "It's Saturday and I've gotten kind of used to you coming by. I have two great bacon, lettuce and tomato sandwiches which I would like to share with you. You have to eat lunch somewhere. And yes, I know you are married. Katie called me and gave me the news. She said the Proposition was still floating in the air."

If I had been eighteen years old this would have been a titillating conversation, but at seventy it made me squirm. I went for the easy out. "I just got through helping Renfroe fix a door at his house and as per usual I did all the work, resulting in my being unfresh and I have leaked sweat all over."

"Jack, I don't care. As a matter of fact, a sweaty man is something I haven't been around in a long time."

I might as well have seen a sign beside the road that said dynamite activity ahead, proceed at your own risk. Had Katie waved the red flag? No, she had not. She was given that opportunity three times last week and did not respond. So, I guess the Proposition lives. "I'll see you in a few minutes."

The door was open and I entered the hallway and heard her voice, "Come on back. I am in the kitchen." I walked on in and she was bent over the counter which reminded me she had a fine ass. "Sit down and have some iced tea, it'll taste good after your hard day at work." The tea had mulled mint leaves and just a hint of sugar. It was delicious.

She turned around. She had on a clean white tee shirt. It was definitely not a leftover from Enos and it defined the teacups as being not empty. She glided over to the chair opposite me and just sat and looked, she did not say a word.

It has always been a mystery to me how some women just have a sexual power that reaches out and touches you. Their pulchritude meter reading doesn't have to be that big a factor. Sometimes it does and sometimes it doesn't. In addition to that, your sexual response bell doesn't always ring from one time to the next. Maryellen is a good example of this. For a year, she was a zero on the attraction scale for me, but for the last two weeks or so, she started to make my clapper active. This sexual response thing also is environmentally sensitive and Maryellen has benefited from that as well, due to her setting the scene. The whole sexual attraction thing changes from girl to girl. Who knows why? Anyhow, as Katie had not dropped the red flag, I could be the choice-maker on this cruise. I could be tied to the whipping post and forced into the redemptive process of bringing color back into Maryellen's rainbow. Or not.

Then she spoke. "Why did you come over here? Curious to find out what might happen if we were left unfettered or are you just being nice to an old sorrow slapped sister? I prefer the first. But, while you are making up your mind, how about that BLT?"

The BLT was amazing, saffron aioli, heirloom tomatoes, butter leaf lettuce and sugar cured bacon cooked just crisp enough. I wondered if there was any correlation between sexual prowess and the ability to make a great sandwich. If there was, I should consider taking a ride on her food truck.

"Actually, I came over her to talk with you," I said "I knew already that you had a confab with Katie and I wanted to know whether you were still on board this expedition?"

"Jack, you know how I feel about Katie. She continues to stand by her contention that I need to be lovingly keelhauled in order to regain my former self. I do admit that I had fun dancing and flirting with you last week and I have looked forward to seeing you again under those same circumstances. Why don't we go into the living room and take up where we left off last Saturday?" I was not given an opportunity to answer in the negative. She took my hand and we walked into the living room.

The room was darker than I remembered and there was a single candle on the mantelpiece. No music yet, we sat and went through the mime routine, same as last week.

"Jack, would you like to dance?" Again, I was timed out on my response and the next sound I heard was Johnny Rivers singing "Swaying to the Music". I remembered seeing him sometime in the sixties at the Whiskey a Go-Go in Atlanta. The dance was slow, smooth, and closer than I remembered. Her head rested gently on my shoulder. Things were moving right along as the song seemed to pave the way for our bodies to weave into each other.

She raised her head from my shoulder and looked at me and said, "Jack, kiss me."

Later that day it would come to me that she never let me answer anything. We did kiss. You have to remember that we were not teenagers. We had participated in moments like this before so it was not a disaster. But it was not like being struck by lightning. So, we tried it again and this time it was better.

Kissing, like painting a picture, is an art and should be treated as such. You have to lay in the background in order for the high points of the painting not to be stark and harsh. Kissing is using the right key to open the front door and then you get to explore and enjoy the whole house.

We easily moved back to the couch. We started to gently explore each other very carefully as if we didn't want to break anything. I don't know why, but my mind flew open and I had one term that was on the big screen in my head, Monkey's Wedding. In Africa, that is what people call it when you have a rain shower and the sun is shining. Somehow what we were doing was like one half of a Monkey Wedding to me. I just didn't know whether it was the rain shower or the sun shining. The sun shone on the immediate activity but a rain cloud covered the whole shebang.

"Maryellen, I have to go, I am starting to see clothes coming off and I am not ready for that." This time I did not let her say anything, I just got up and walked out. I was as sure as I could ever be about anything. She understood.

I wondered if it was coincidence that I walked out into the rain, but the sun was not shining, so the chances of it being omenish was small. Got into my truck and rolled away. I had gone at least three blocks before I realized where I was. I am always amazed when that happens, and I wonder why I was not wrecked into a big tree. I wasn't thinking about anything. Just a big blank in my thought process. I knew Katie was home and I wondered what my reception would be. I had already prepared my answer to the 'for sure' question I would be asked. Probably not at first, but soon after my arrival. It would come like a heat seeking missile.

PORN STARS

I OPENED THE DOOR to total silence. That was a bad sign. Music was a constant in our house, especially if Katie was there alone. Television was an anathema to her smooth being. There were exceptions. One of the royal family getting married, a president dying, or Neal Young being on Austin City Limits. The light was bright and there she was, sitting on the sofa, but sitting as if she was in a straight-backed chair. She was wearing black jeans, a gray polo shirt, bare footed with super scarlet toe nails. Going with the often bad strategy that the best defense is a good offense, I strode into the room and announced, as if I had a bullhorn, "I would love a good steak tonight. Your choice. Go out or cook in."

The only problem with doing this is that Katie could see through me like I was made of blown glass. Look out for the missile.

"Jack, have you been to Maryellen's?"

Staying tight with my conversion to the church of honesty I humbly said. "Yes." Things were not copacetic. I did not want to but I had to turn and look at her.

"Well," she said," What level of chumminess did you two achieve this fine Saturday? Did you earn any merit badges for sexual godliness or was it just plain old rutting?",

Well at least she did not drop the Marriage Bomb and ask "Do you realize you are a married man now?"

The stillness in the room could have caused cancer. It was shattered like broken crystal by the easy to recognize sound of someone bouncing a basketball on the sidewalk in front of our house. May God bless that child.

"I have to know," she said. "It has been revealed to me that I may have overestimated my depth of understanding. I thought I could handle it, but now I'm not so sure. I want to know what happened."

When someone you know has done something you knew was wrong from the gitgo and they had just a tad of righteousness thrown in for good measure, sometimes a golden opportunity is born. Then when it all starts to leak a little, it is hard not to twist the knife just a fraction. At least smack them across the head with an "I told you so." But, the initiator of this hot mess was my best buddy, lover, and wife all rolled into one. I passed on the knife and the "I told you so."

I spoke like I was a Supreme Court justice. "A better question would be, is Maryellen making some progress. Has the interaction between her and a genteel geezer like myself caused her to reconsider whether she should remain in her re-virgin era. As for answering your question, she is still a re-virgin, but is starting to question the validity of her chastity. Katie, you will always have two best friends, Jack and Maryellen. We still are not fully on board with your concept, but we are willing to try and produce a positive conclusion and at the same time not to expose our Amicus Curiae as an idiot."

I could tell I had just recorded a 'strike- em out, throw- em out' right there in our living room. Katie smiled as only she could smile. If she was a heavenly body the sun would be out of a job.

"C'mere baby." She said these two words as only she could. I wanted to remain still and pat myself on the back, but when she spoke her voice came out like it was mingled with tiny pebbles causing very thin cracks in the sound and I had no defense.

The next thing I knew, I was sitting on the couch with Katie and we were both naked, except for socks. Like we were posing for an over the hill porn movie. I knew what would happen next. Both of us started laughing like hell. Then we pounced on each other and rolled around like two Go-rillas for a few more seconds. After more laughing, she said, "You know that song that Enos was always writing? Nekkid Dancing? It is time to put it to good use. Music, my man. Let's dance."

Beth Hart flowed into the room as only she could, singing, "Tell

Her You Belong to Me." The dancing flowed like wine from a decanted bottle of a delicate vintage.

Later that night, we ate bruschetta made with Cherokee pink tomatoes which paired well with an Italian red. Both of us still held on to a sex glowstick. She had on navy blue silk pants with a light blue tee shirt top. She shimmered.

Katie spoke. "I guess I should call Maryellen and thank her for doing such a good job of fluffing on you. I just might send you over there every time I feel the need." I said nothing. "C'mon Jack, the danger has passed us by. You can tell me what happened today, how many rungs up the ladder did you and my best friend climb? I have a feeling that you did not get up on the roof."

I did not want to tell her anything. Today had not been an entry level event. I had seen the green monster rear its ugly head when I got home. It was not pleasant. I was convinced that Katie eventually would be unable to harness the jealousy horse. When that happened, heartache would combine with tribulation to be served in equal portions all around.

I cast my lot with brevity. "Today we kissed and medium petting occurred. Nakedness never made an entrance. Not even one button was disturbed, it was not even close." Ok, I could feel comfortable that I had told the truth, but real truth is provisioned with color from a large palette and passion from way down deep. I had talked like an old movie in black and white. The entire room was suddenly black and white. Such a shame. The good time had disappeared and it was not playing hide and seek. It was gone.

I leaned over the counter and gave her a small kiss and walked out of the room. I have been doing a lot of walking out of rooms lately and I did not like it.

I was in the bed alone for a while, but Katie padded into the room barefoot and cuddled up to me and said these words. "It's okay Jack, we are okay. We are an opus and no skinny little big nosed librarian can take us off the shelf. We are good and will be good forever." We went to sleep with the still alive gloom. But for the time being, it was on life support.

TOLIVER

IT WAS SUNDAY MORNING and Maryellen crept from her bed and walked into the kitchen. She made herself a cup of coffee, tuned in the Revivalists on Spotify and did a small dance turn in her kitchen. What to eat? Not much. She was skipping in the sunshine and it felt good. The widow was drenched in a feeling that she had not experienced in a long time. She sat down at the breakfast bar and considered her renaissance. What else could it be? She had dreamed about kissing someone, but it was like watching the middle of a movie with no beginning or end.

Had the Katie proposal rolled away the stone? When was the last time I got up in the morning and danced by myself in the kitchen? It was longer than I could remember. I walked to the window, the weather was paying me a big compliment by exhibiting nothing but blue skies and bright sun. Slow down, just enjoy it for a little while, nothing really happened yesterday with Jack. One big breakout kiss and then a further excursion into the world of teen age petting. It was fun and I have to admit, if Jack had not trotted his ass out of there, there might have been a more significant event. A brief reversion to sexual exploration. I thought to myself, this is progress and I am going to bathe in it as much as possible. I think I actually saw a flash of pink in the world of Maryellen.

The library was open on Sunday afternoon. She did not usually go in on Sunday, but one of her assistants had requested the day off, so she was going in to cover for her. The trip to the library was strange. She still was listening to the Revivalists and it was like they knew of her progression in provenance and were congratulating her with music appropriate for the moment. The library was usually not busy on Sunday afternoons. High school students striving to finish a paper due on Monday morning. Cheapos coming in to read the New York Times. Maryellen used times like this to catch up on some paperwork. She was working in her office and had done a lot of ordinary stuff, when she realized she needed to take a break.

She walked up to the desk and was in quiet conversation with Deandre about the repositioning of books in the children's section, when a male voice made a breakthrough to Maryellen. "Ma'am, do you have a new collection of short stories by Thomas McGuane called Cloudburst?"

Maryellen started to defer the question to Deandre without looking at the voice, but the question was quickly followed by another. "Aren't you Maryellen?"

Before she could answer, he continued, "You might not remember me, we went to high school together many long years ago. You look the same. I have changed from large to not so large. My name is Toliver Gordon. We took biology together."

Maryellen slowly looked toward him and she thought to herself, that is the whitest man I have ever seen and yes, I do remember him being in my biology class. The teacher was a football coach and only taught the class due to his having to teach something and they had nobody else to rattle on about protozoas. It was plain to us that he had no idea about anything but H backs and triple options. We even called him coach. Toliver and I shared a table and I remembered him as being very smart, I thought he should have been teaching the class. We both made A's. "Yes, I do remember you, are you still smart?"

Now how stupid was that, she thought. They both laughed and he said "Smarter".

"To answer your question, we do have the book in reference, I'll get it for you."

She returned with the book and he said, "Thank you, and it was good to run into you again." He walked off to a big chair in the back. Maryellen thought it was strange that he was going to stay in the library to read until she remembered the book was a collection of short stories. He could read some, then leave. She could not help herself as she checked him out as he walked to the chair. He walked in a strange rolling manner, like he was expecting the floor to move and he needed absolute control over his limbs. His belly was small and not one that protected his privates. He still had that white, white hair. Immediately, realization flooded her brain that she had not taken inventory of a male since old what's his name died. That had to be progress. She returned to her office.

Maryellen went back to her tasks, but she had not done much when Deandre poked her head around the door, "Maryellen," she said, "The man at the front wants to talk with you.

She wondered what in the heck he wanted as she walked back to the front. "Maryellen," he asked, "What time does the library close?"

"Four o'clock" was her reply.

"Would you like a cup of coffee or tea? I'd like to catch up. I haven't been back in town for too long."

Surprise dripped off her face like a warm popsicle. What to do? Maryellen said. "Sure, give me thirty minutes. You should be able to finish the first story in the book." She did not remember returning to her office, and only became unaddled upon sitting in her chair. Speaking to herself in the third person, she said, "Calm down. This is not a date. This is just a cup of coffee and conversation."

Under normal circumstances, she would have called Katie and said," You will never guess what just happened." But now that level of friendship was under duress and she felt a ding of sadness. The good thing about it was that it did not concern Enos. Enos could not be fixed, but her friendship with Katie still had a chance of redemption.

She compromised, and sent her a text.

"Katie, a real man just asked me out for a cup of coffee. Do not start whipping yourself on the back, and hopping up and down like a seven-year old girl playing hopscotch. This is just a small step for Maryellen kind, and, yes, I am going."

Tolliver was waiting at the door when she came out to close up. She took another gander at him just to make sure he hadn't lost a limb or become disfigured in some way. He hadn't. The early sunshine had retired to be replaced by big busomy gray clouds and small droplets of rain They stood in the small entry alcove and looked at each other in a wary manner. Maryellen thought to herself, he had been married and his wife died way to soon. She just knew it. There had been much water under both their bridges. There was lots to talk about.

"There is a very good coffee shop just about a half block away," Maryellen volunteered. "Do you mind walking a little in the rain? If not, there is a small non-franchise coffee shop right down there." She pointed it out.

"My sugar coating has been gone for a while, so let's do it," answered Toliver.

After the short walk in the rain, they sat and both ordered a vanilla latte. Toliver picked up the ball and ran with it. "I am going to offer up a suggestion. Why don't we start with our current situations and go backward to birth? This is the first time I have been in the immediate company of a female in a while."

Maryellen caught the lateraled ball and said. "Let me guess, you are a recent widower. I joined that club about a year ago and my social skills are coated with rust."

Toliver wore disbelief like a newfound talent and his answer was febrile to say the least. "How did you know that? Did I send signals like a third base coach?"

Maryellen started to laugh and almost caught a guffaw before it escaped her mouth but was unsuccessful and it exploded the nervous tension at the table and made them both comfortable. "No, I wasn't laughing at you, I was laughing because I used that same phrase in talking with my best friend recently. I can't recall the exact circumstances, but I said did I send signals like a third base coach. The problem with saying that to her is that she had no idea what I was talking about. I, on the other hand, had a dad who loved baseball and I was lucky enough for that to be my most valued inheritance. I take it that you are a fan also."

His answer was, "The New York Yankees are my team and always will be."

In that small bit of repartee, the pending imbroglio was nothing but a danger dispensed and they entered into a relaxed review of their respective lives. Toliver was a widower of fourteen months. They had been married thirty-eight years. He was a retired naval officer, loved music, could speak a little French, had one son who sold fertilizer in north Mississippi. Toliver had decided to move back home about a year after she died, because he did not have a place, he could call home except here. Being in the Navy, he was afloat a lot of the time and therefore was gone for long stretches. Now he knows what it was like for her while he was deployed, except she was not coming back.

Maryellen came clean about her life. Librarian, no kids, best friend Katie, loves music, reads a lot, hates politics and so on and so forth. An observer watching this unfold would have surmised that they were a couple who had been long together and still liked each other. There was laughing, poking each other on the arm, one of them recounting an old story that they both knew and still enjoyed. No cells were answered or google googled. They were having a grand time.

The bottom of the latte cups had been showing for at least a half hour when Toliver got up and scooted around the table and helped her exit the chair. He got chivalry points.

Walking through the door, they discovered the rain had disappeared and they sauntered up the street to their cars. He said, "A Demain."

She said, "Maybe not tomorrow but soon," and smiled like a little girl.

SUNDAY DINNER

THE K'S ARRIVED AROUND three Sunday afternoon.

Katie, Kasein and Kalia immediately formed a three-person symbiosis that was impenetrable for any male on this earth. I assumed the position of waiter. I wonder if this is what I am faced with the rest of my life. I would be like an appendix. I was in the body, but was of no use and had no function. Oh well.

Katie had enough clothes for an entire first grade but they were all for Kalia. She had bought her the complete set of Nancy Drew books. I had asked earlier, if they were not too advanced for Kalia. No, Katie answered, I could tell she was way ahead of her grade in school she will read these with ease. Kasein was also the recipient of stuff, black dress, shoes, workout clothes. She was adept in the good manners of accepting a gift with grace, something that is not practiced nearly enough. I was completely ignored, I felt like a wart.

By dinners end, the conversation level to a stranger would have been judged to be a family of decades. Laughter, soft insults, sarcasms were present just like any happy family. I did not want them to leave, but Kasein had work and Kalia had school. I knew this was going to be a good thing. Katie was ecstatic, as they drove off, she grabbed my hand, nuzzled me with her chin and said, "Thank you Jack for including me in this, you could have made it all about you and Kasein and left me out in the cold. But you made sure that I was involved. You trusted me to accept your past and I will always love you for that trust. We are going to be good forever."

During the walk to the door, Jack had leaned over to speak to

Kasein, "Could I meet you one afternoon this week. We have not had a chance to talk, just you and I."

Kasein seemed eager to answer, "What about tomorrow at four? If you could come to my house. That would be good. Kalia has gymnastics from 3 till 5."

MARYELLE CONTINUES

HAD KATIE BEEN RIGHT and prescribed the right medicine? Was Jack the poultice that provided an entry back into the world of the living and loving? Maryellen still had the smile on her face as she drove home. She was also wise enough not to declare this a home run. But it was at least a bunt single and she was on her way to first base.

It was fun and she scratched the itch to talk with Katie. Maryellen jumped right in with both feet and she led off with, "I know you are sitting by the phone wanting all the dirty details." Most of the time hellos were abandoned between them.

"Actually, Kasein and Kalia just walked out the door, I was just sitting down to call you."

"Well there are no dirty details. I just had a cup of coffee down at the coffee shop by the library and we had a great time. He is a recent widower, just a little longer than me. Retired Naval officer. Tolliver Gordon is his name. Our age, a music lover. Come to think of it, I don't think I have ever gone out with a man that you could reverse his names as first or last names. I need to look that up tomorrow and see if there is a term for it. He is nice guy. Go ahead and ask. I know what your first question will be."

Katie did not hesitate, "Of course you know, what does he look like? Does he have that mid body fat flap? Does he have his own teeth? Does he walk with good posture, and does not do that old person shuffle? Bald headed or have a good head of gray hair? Does he have gorilla hair on his back, but I guess you don't know that yet? If he has one of those combover things you have to dump him immediately... Gimme the details."

Maryellen had a good warm interior laugh that felt like drinking hot chocolate. "Well, the physical details are thus. In general, he is the whitest man I have ever seen. His hair is still majorly white but with a bestrewal of light gray. Good teeth, great posture, probably a by-product of his military history. No combover, very small belly, certainly not a big negative. All in all, a good solid B plus/ A minus. He has aged well. No whisky nose or cigarette lines and he smelled good."

The conversation continued and followed the time indentured rules of female to female dissection of a first interaction with a male. Questions were answered as to when the next rendezvous would occur, where it would occur, when was he going to call and so on and so forth.

All was well with Katie and Maryellen. Then the mood changed as Katie broke the skin with a knife-like question: "Am I to tell Jack he is no longer needed as you have gotten out of intensive care, and from this point forward you will be okay with self-administered rehab?"

This ambuscade was successful in converting the color of the conversation from bright yellows and pinks to cerulean at best. Maryellen felt as if she were paddling a kayak serenely and happily on a late Sunday afternoon and suddenly was upside down under the water. Her first reaction was that she was pissed. The term 'concentrated bitch' went across her big screen like a cheetah. The words came out of her mouth in a stumblin bumblin stream, "I haven't decided yet. Tell Jack I will be in touch." Goodbyes passed each other like long time strangers.

JACK AND KASEIN CONVERSE

KASEIN SAT AT HER kitchen table. What does he want to talk about?

Jack drove slowly, as he was having an internal discussion between Jack the Person and Jack the Father. Just as he came to stop in front of her house, he decided that they both wanted to get the same thought across to her.

Her house was small but efficient, two stories with a chimney. It was painted a forest green with yellow trim. Lots of shrubbery and small trees. The back yard was encased by a wood privacy fence, Jack could see a couple of citrus trees off to one side. Jack was impressed.

Kasein opened the door before he could knock. "Come in. Would you like a cup of coffee, I have some chocolate chip oatmeal cookies. They are my favorite. I hope you like them. I thought we might sit at the kitchen table." All of this poured out like a prepared speech. She was almost out of breath when she finished.

"A cup of coffee would be great. I have never had oatmeal chocolate chip cookies, but I have found that if you put enough chocolate chips in a cookie, almost any kind of cookie would be good. The kitchen table is a good suggestion." They sat down, coffee was served and both had a cookie in hand.

Jack started, "Kasein, when you think about it, we don't know each other from Adam. You have had a little longer to digest what I just found out last week. But, both of us are still in the startup stage of expanding our families. I have put in a lot of time trying to decide my course of action in being a father. I do not believe that parents automatically deserve love from their child and vice versa. The gentleman that raised you as a father is someone that I owe a major debt of gratitude. Obviously, he did a great job. I have made this decision; I am going to treat you as the adult you are. I hope that you and I can progress in this build process and will hold hands in the end. I hope you understand the conversation I just completed. I guess the bottom line is that when two people are dancing for the first time. They don't want to step on each other's toes. And call me Jack."

Kasein released a small smile across her face. "Jack, If I had started this conversation, you would have thought that I had prior knowledge of your thoughts. The path you have charted is good with me. I asked for us to get together, but do you have something in particular that you want to discuss or are we just getting to know each other?"

Jack took a bite of cookie and assumed the countenance of someone finally deciding on what he wanted to say. "A little of both, but let's get the ugly part out on the table. You are the only person to know what I am about to tell you and that includes Katie. I had a meeting with my doctor a short time ago and was informed that I was on the last lap of the race. I have a heart condition called hypertrophic obstructive cardiomyopathy, otherwise known as HOCM. There is no cure, I was born with it. It is a thickening of the heart that inhibits the heart from pumping enough blood to the body. Most cases, it is sudden and permanent. I did not tell Katie because I want our remaining time to be as normal as possible. I have a little pain, shortness of breath, and some other stuff. It came to me that you were sent to me as a sort of blessing, someone I could confide in about this whole thing."

Jack stopped and looked at Kasein. He had expected consternation at the very least, but had not expected the tears that ran down her cheeks in small rivulets. To him. her face read sadness, understanding and an ironical smile. He did not know what to say, so he shut up.

Kasein did not hesitate, "Did you also know that it is hereditary. If your parent has it, you have a fifty percent chance to have it. Would you care to guess which half of that equation I fall into?

"I have it also. After my mom died, I had a complete checkup. I don't have cancer leanings but I do have HOCM. That is one of the reasons I looked you up. Over the recent past, I have come to accept my death as a task that I have to get ready for. The first entry on my task list is Kalia. I have no relatives, except one whiskey addled half-brother. You are my only still walking kin folk. I was hoping that you were not bestricken. We are common carriers. I had Kalia tested, she is not."

Kasein's voice strengthened and she continued. "I told Renfroe that I did not want to disturb your life or lay claim to your money. I was not completely honest. I was looking for someone who could take care of Kalia, if I pass on."

Jack stood up, walked around the table and put his arms out. Kasein rose and they hugged like it was a familiar event, but this time it was special.

Jack then took the chair next to her and said, "I am not the person, who could fill that billet, but I might know someone who could. I will talk with her when I get home."

The conversation flowed into tributaries of a much happier nature. Music was discussed, they were compatible. Food, he likes to eat, she likes to cook. Education, she went to Florida State, he had gone to Florida. Reading, he likes spy books, she likes biographies. There were no major divergences that could not be handled.

Jack was given a bag of cookies to take to Katie. Another trip home that did not let him just ride along and listen to music. How was he going to deliver this package of news to Katie? He did not want to expose her to his news just Kasein's. Again, he fell back on his latterly approach to communication with Katie. He might start his conversation with that old saying, "Truth be told"

Jack strode into his house that was dimly lit. He detected movement in the kitchen and eased into that area. Katie was standing next to the counter top, dressed for bed. She was as beautiful as a chilled glass of sancerre. She was unaware of Jack, so he did not move and continued to enjoy the scene before him. She slowly rotated her body around the room as if she was a dancer and picked up on Jack's presence. "Hey Baby, where you been?"

Jack did not mind the dying part, but what really pissed him off was the loss of times like these.

"I have been to Kasein's to talk with her. Jack had decided to change things a little bit due to not wanting to get his health situation on the table. Last night she said she would like for the two of us to have an opportunity to just sit and talk. Come to find out, she had a particular subject in mind. It turns out that her appearance in our lives did have more of a purpose than what has been revealed to us prior to today. Can I make you a drink? I am going to have one."

Katie asked, "What are you having?"

"Bourbon and water with a twist of lemon fits the bill for me."

"Make it two and let's go sit on the couch. Do we need music?"

Jack spoke back over his should as he mixed the drinks. "For once, no music."

Jack sat down on the sofa and placed Katie's drink on the table top next to her. She sat with her back to the end of the sofa and extended her legs over Jack's lap.

After a light swallow of the drink. Jack said, "You remember Kasein's mother died of cancer and during the dying process, her mother told Kasein the name of her biological father. Her mother's death of cancer and the potential hereditary connection pushed Kasein into having a complete medical exam. The results being, Kasein has a disease, I can't remember the exact name, but it is a heart disease, no cure and she could die at anytime. She has no relatives except for an unreliable brother. Her appeal to us is that if something happens to her, you and I step in and make sure that Kalia is in good hands. As I understand it, she is not asking us to take care of her, just for us to make sure she is okay." He stopped and looked at Katie for a response.

Jack knew he had not been forthright with Katie. She did not know that there was good possibility that this request would fall entirely into her hands. She would be responsible for Kalia's wellbeing, because Jack might be in Tennessee. Jack felt small drops of regret rain fall but selfishly did not say anything to change the situation.

"Jack, we have enough money, our health is good, we don't travel much and we have never had the responsibility of being a parent. I think it is time for us to step up. I don't think we should be responsible for getting Kalia in the right place. I think we should be responsible for Kalia all day, every day. We have good friends who could contribute time and talent. I think it would be not only great, but it is the right thing to do. Tomorrow, you should talk with Kasein. Tell her we will be the parental figures if needed, if it is good with her. If she is ok with that, you should call your kayak buddy and have him draw up the necessary documents." She leaned back against the sofa, took a big girl gulp of her drink and smiled.

DINNER AT TOLLIVER'S

A COUPLE OF DAYS slunk by with nothing happening at all. Wednesday morning Maryellen was sitting at her desk and her cell phone rang. She did not recognize the number. She had not heard from Katie and was just as glad that she hadn't, but this call was not her. She picked up the phone and "Hello."

The response was "This is Tolliver. How are you this fine morning?"

Underneath her breath she sighed, whew. He did call. "I am fine. How are you?".

"Good, very good. I know you're busy and I've been practicing my short request, would you like to have dinner tonight? I am actually a fair cook and I'd like to demonstrate my culinary skills to one of the local elite. Please feel free to tell me that food is not your thing. To some people it just functions as fuel. My son is like that. If you enjoy the palatable process, please come and share a meal with me."

Maryellen liked the open invite and put a plus mark by his name. "What time should I be there and what can I bring?"

"How about you bring a salad. Salads should be pretty and cold. They are not part of my skill set. Six o'clock would be good but that is flexible if it would jam you up from leaving work."

Maryellen in a cocky manner, said "See you then," and hung up the phone. Anyone watching her walk across the room would say, "Maryellen's body language sent out the message, "I've still got the goods."

Salad, what salad should it be? My watchword should be non-pretentious, but not just lettuce and tomatoes. Should I call and ask what he is cooking, so I could match up? But he was taking a chance on his selection. So, would I. I thought salade nicoise but that is up there on the pretentious scale. I will have to stop off at the store. The decision is for plain with chickpeas, red and yellow bell peppers, cherry tomatoes, cucumber, green onions, feta cheese, avocado, and a basic basil vinaigrette. Put it in a big bowl and call it done.

His house was in older section of town. The small pale yellow house dwarfed by a big oak tree in a tiny front yard was a grace to its surroundings. It was all wood, with a well-used swing on the front porch. Small green fence around the back of the house. An all brick patio covered most of the backyard.

He opened the door as I walked up the steps. Music engulfed me as I entered the living room, which actually extended into the small kitchen. There were wooden stairs off to one side. A small library lined one wall and two original paintings flecked the other side of the room. The first words out of my mouth were, "You are a fan of the Revivalists, I listened to them to start my day."

He replied, "I debated all afternoon about the music, so I ended up playing one of my recent favorites, only to discover now that they are one of yours also." Maryellen thought, that sounds like my thought progression on salads. Toliver picked up where he left off, "They have several songs I like, Wish I knew You, Soul Fight, Got Love. They are not a new group. Let me say, you have free license to make changes anytime you hear a song you don't like. I'm going to declare myself eclectic when it comes to music. I am not a fan of bluegrass or new rap. Other than those two, I can probably go with anything.

"Can I get you a glass of wine? I have a pretty good bottle of pinot noir opened.".

Maryellen found herself drawn to the house as if she had been born there. Her body felt stress and tension fall around her feet like wax from a burning candle. The music playing was, "Soulfight". She began a slow twirl to the music and felt a small smile take residence on her face.

Toliver caught the smile, interpreted it with ease like it was writing in the air and said, "I feel the same way about this house, I decided to buy it as soon as I drove up, while still seated in the car. The entire setting said home to me."

Maryellen took the glass of wine from Tolliver. She felt his little finger lightly graze her little finger as if to say "Hello."

"What are we eating, my salad is designed to match up with just about anything."

He replied "Steak tournedos with a mushroom sauce and a vodka penne." He casually added, "Just a little something I threw together at the last minute."

During the meal, which bordered on sublime, the conversation flowed commensurate with the wine drunk. Maryellen was having a fine old time. The food and wine painted a picture with great colors, not grays or blacks. She asked, "Tell me something about you in the present that might cause a non- believer to look askance at you upon telling it."

His mind turned inward searching for a candidate to relate to Maryellen. "I was driving the other day listening to "Wish I Knew You Then," and found myself moving around in the car seat and making my arms slowly wave like snakes with joints, and it occurred to me that there should be a contest, Car Seat Dancing. Almost all musicatos do it. We all have our 'go to' moves with our hands, so why not have a contest. I am sure television would pick it up, judges and everything. There would be rules, you would have to keep at least one hand on the steering wheel, one cheek of your butt must touch the seat at all times. You could have lights that would come on and loud noises like donkeys braying when contact was broken with the seat and you would be disqualified. What do you think?"

Maryellen did not know what to say. Her powers of reasoning had been seasoned with the pinot noir, but she said, "I think it's a grand idea. You could have couples dancing by incorporating the passenger." Then she thought to herself, now that is a stupid comment but appropriate for his suggestion.

Maryellen felt herself to be a harmonic caused by someone or something touching her as a musical string producing an exquisite note. It had been a long time since she had put feet on this path.

She carefully slowed the vibration and asked another question.

"Tell me something about yourself from your past, something of significance to you, something that is more important to you than others might realize."

Tolliver looked away and when he turned back, his face had been resurfaced, as smooth and sad as an old road. When he spoke, it was in the voice of someone from far away who could not be reached. "When I was in the Naval Academy, I played football. I was the blocking back. I did not get to run the ball much, but I was the facilitator for our running game. The scatback was Cecil Howard. The term scatback has died a death by modernization. Cecil was my roommate; he was about five feet six inches tall and weighed about one hundred fifty-five pounds. He was my roommate from my first day until my last day. He was a black man. I was six feet two inches tall, weighed two hundred and twenty pounds and I was and still am a white man. He was from Michigan. I was from here. I don't understand it but from the first thirty seconds of our meeting we were best friends, like brothers. We went everywhere together. Our lockers were adjacent and our friendship was a binding that helped alleviate all of the hellish stuff that went on especially as plebes. He was the best man at my wedding and vice versa. We were given the name Antipodes within the first half of our first year and it stuck.

"Upon graduation I went on a battleship and he went into the Seals. Long story short, he died on a combat mission. He was on a sniper team, out in the boonies for three days without movement. One of his teammates attracted attention from a Vietnamese sniper and Cecil was shot from long distance. I will never forget the message I received while cruising in the Pacific from his spotter. "Cecil Howard died today in service of his country. He said to tell you goodbye." The voice grew in timbre as he brought this memory from its grave. "Actually, the name Antipodes was not entirely accurate. We both craved competition, we loved football, and had unlimited honor and respect for the U.S. Navy, especially the Academy."

Tolliver reached over and picked up his glass and took a swallow as if it were an unction for the pain. Maryellen felt as if she had been allowed entry into the vault of a man's soul.

Maryellen knew that the curtain had dropped on the evening, she also realized she was holding hands with Tolliver. Maryellen knew she was going down the rabbit hole, but it was too quick for her. She got up and asked if she could help clear and clean. He said no he would take care of it. She quickly said, "I have to work tomorrow." She leaned over and gave him a quick kiss on the top of his white hair and said goodbye.

Maryellen stretched out in her bed later that night, listening to the Cowboy Junkies do, "When We Arrive", a song that fit this night like a bespoke suit. Mentally she assessed the night as if she was a theater critic for the New York Times. *I implore all serious thespians to avoid the current production of Maryellen and Tolliver. Tolliver was okay, he did not hurt anybody. Maryellen, however, was painful to watch. She reminded me of a young giraffe and her departing scene was a disgrace to the art of theater.... No style, no grace, just get the hell out of dodge. She knew she was not ready for the dramatic.*

Maryelllen thought she would like to have something with another human, but she felt as if she had been on the sex wagon for so long, she would not remember how. When she realized they were holding hands, she panicked as she thought he might do the old lean in for a kiss. He had not, but she pulled on the bridle hard enough to keep from just running out, but still making an atrocious exit.

Her actions with Jack had been like pouring milk from a bottle. "Easy as pie" as her mother would say. Why is that she wondered? The evening had not been some bizarre freak show? Then it came to her like an arrow into a bullseye. She had been all shits and giggles the entire early part of the evening, when the screenplay was still a comedy. As soon as Tolliver talked about the Antipodes, the comedy crawled into a corner and died. Drama was at the top of the marquee. Someone had stuck a stick in the spokes. It was as plain as having a wart on her face. She was not ready for any serious stuff, but she wanted to. She needed to be side by side with someone.

Thinking about it, she reconsidered Katie's Proposition. Maybe she needed to be weaned from this sorrow thing. She decided to call Jack in the morning. She coasted into a deep cavern of sleep, accompanied by Macie Gray singing "Why Didn't You Call Me."

JACK AND KATIE

IN A HOUSE NEARBY, two people sat across from each other on their deck. There was no conversation, both of them had a glass of wine in their respective hands. Katie spoke softly to her companion. "Jack, I have talked with Kasein and Kalia every day this week. Today Kasein and I had a long conversation, mainly discussing our decision to step in as grandparents of Kalia, in case something happens to Kasein. I will tell you this, Ms. Kasein does not skate around important questions. She wades into the deep water without hesitation. We talked about our age, which is a valid concern. I told her that we have friends who would help us at any time. We also talked about you and I not having worn the parental gowns. I started to be a smartass and say something like, 'Well how hard can it be?' But I recognized that morsel of humor would not be swallowed well at all. Kasein suggested we keep Kalia for short periods of time that would lead to longer visits, it would be good for all three of us. I can't remember it all, but you get the general idea that we had a thorough discussion. The bottom line is that she is okay with our being parents to Kalia. Jack, I cannot sit on this too much longer. How about we have a party Friday night, with the usual group and introduce our two new relatives to everyone at once?"

Jack answered and spoke with a smile perched on his face like a bird on a wire. "Thank you for the suggestion. I have been thinking about the unveiling all day today. I think that would be a stupendous event. Kasein and Kalia could spend the night."

THE PARTY

MARYELLEN AND TOLLIVER WERE hand in hand as they left her car and strolled up the sidewalk, they had the demeanor of movie stars walking up the red carpet and blowing kisses to people in the audience. This was Friday night. On Thursday night Maryellen had called Tolliver and apologized for her leaving his house like an escaped convict. She had adopted Jack's practice of using an honest paintbrush on all surfaces. It was easier.

"Tolliver, I would like to extend an apology for my hasty withdrawal Wednesday night. I could feel myself being drawn into a neck of the woods I was not quite ready for. Anyway, Katie just called and invited you and me to dinner tomorrow night. So, I am asking you out on a date. If you want to go, I'll pick you up about six o'clock."

Tolliver spent a few candid points in his reply. "Maryellen, you have to know that if we keep hanging out together, eventually we are going to press our lips together and expose ourselves to that big decision of who is going to be on top. To answer your invitation, I would be delighted as a turtle who made it across the road to accompany the potentially libidinous librarian to the party." She laughed and hung up.

They rang the doorbell in the midst of a discussion about the value of listening to a baseball game on the radio with Dizzy Dean as one of the announcers. Jack opened the door and in typical Jack fashion, he said "Maryellen, who is this better looking version of Andy Warhol you picked up?"

"Jack, this is Tolliver Gordon, formerly of the U.S. Navy and newly arrived to live in his old home town. No, we have not had sex, so put that question back in your pocket."

As the conversation weakened, up strolled Cherie and Trip. Cherie lifted her nose as if sniffing the air. "I smell indecency. It is prevalent. It is strong as Charles Atlas. Don't let us be the man on the side of a construction site with a sign that says stop, please continue the discourse. Or has the conversation run its natural course? Move over, I am going in. It is Friday night and I am going to find the hidden cache of tequila. C'mon Trip, leave this tripod of open mouths. By the way, no one passed out an intro of the big, good looking man holding the hand of Miss Maryellen." Without waiting for the intro, she disappeared into the house with Trip in tow.

Katie just appeared, as if she were a guest on a late night TV show. "Hello folks, c'mon in and let me make you a drink. This must be Tolliver. Maryellen, on first glance you have done well by yourself. I am Katie, long suffering aficionado of Miss Maryellen and her misguided ways." And the door closed behind them.

Not one attendee of the party knew that across the street in the front seat of a white pickup truck there was a, let's call it a discussion, going on between Renfroe and Ruby. Said Ruby in a formal manner, "Renfroe, I know I saw Jack going into Maryellen's house last Saturday and he was in there a long while. I was across the street taking a class in embroidered jewelry. I was not stalking or spying. It just happened. I know you know what's going on, you and Jack and that stupid Kayak Talk thing you do. C'mon, give it up. If you give it up, you might receive something in reciprocation later tonight."

Renfroe looking for leverage, said "Would the reciprocal include some ancillaries?"

Ruby hesitated as if she was a financial analyst calculating the risk reward ratio. "Depends on the juiciness of the storyline."

Renfroe sat straight up in his seat and made the decision that any red blooded eighteen-year old boy would. "Ruby, this is KayakTalk, so you cannot tell anyone that I gave it up like a French prisoner, but this is double inside stuff. Long story short, Katie offered up Jack to Maryellen as a passageway back to a more convivial life and that's all I know. I do not know which step of the stairway to heaven they are on or if they still have all four feet flat on the ground. Now that is all I am going to say."

Ruby cogitated for a good long minute and asked a question, "If you die and I act really sad, will Katie offer to loan me Jack? What do you think?"

Renfroe sometimes talked a good game but it was well known that his love for Ruby was made of cast iron and he never strayed outside the base lines. That old story about the guy who finally fools around on his wife and then goes home and brags about it, that might be Renfroe. "Ruby, I love you with both feet and Jack is one of my best friends, so I will make a pre-departure plead: Don't do it." They got out of the truck and walked across the street holding hands.

The party had stepped up a notch as the Rooks invaded but had not approached a besotted level. Drinks inhabited every other hand and happiness floated like soap bubbles in the air.

Jack, being somewhat of a religious agnostic, always loved to poke the bear, the bear being Renfroe. He spoke above the crowd. "Renfroe, are you still going to that same church, or are you dissatisfied that too many of the women are wearing dresses that provide no glimpse of cleavage? I have a new church for you. I saw it the other day, the Apoplectic, Apostolic Temple of the Apocalypse. Sounds like a combination of snake handlers, talking in tongues, healing hands and rock and roll junkies. What do you think? It's got to have good music."

Renfroe spoke just as he was just accosting his first beverage. "Sounds okay to me except for the snake part. I don't like snakes and have a definite preference to shooting them as opposed to handling them."

Katie leaped from her chair like a cheerleader who still had the enthusiasm and forever smile but one whose body had gone head to head with sixty-five years. "Maryellen, tell us about your man. You have the floor for three minutes, then it will be open for questions from the press."

Maryellen took the floor like a pro. "Tolliver has moved back to his beginnings. We took the same biology course in high school. I re-met Mr. Tolliver Gordon in the library last Sunday afternoon. He is a graduate of the U.S. Naval Academy and recently retired from that branch of service. He is a music man, a great cook, has a creative mind that is engaged at all times and enjoys a good laugh. He has one son and he wears a size thirteen shoe. From what I've seen he has all his fingers and toes. I will take questions for a short time as I have a cabinet meeting in five minutes."

Tolliver stood, drink in hand. Bourbon by the way. "I would like to post a short addendum to my bio, which by the way was an excellent presentation. In the Navy she would have been much appreciated as a person who squeezed off bullet points and did not waste time with non- matters. It is a pleasure to be in the midst of a group that totally practices all three types of friendship ...Utility, pleasure and good. That is according to Aristotle. He also said friendship is a slow ripening fruit."

The air just froze until Jack jumped up and said, "Two minutes in the penalty box for a too serious addendum."

And the party resumed. The food was great. Steak and baked potato with stuff all in it. Garlic bread and a salad of cucumbers, lettuce and green olives. The dessert was always the same with this group... A large container of vanilla ice cream was placed on the table accompanied by a can of whipped cream. A big plate with many home baked brownies topped with thick icing and a new bottle of Hershey's chocolate syrup completed the lineup. Everyone made their own version and it was impossible to screw it up.

Conversations were heard about the latest baseball trades, politics of course, and the all-time winner at gatherings of mature adults, the latest visit to a doctor. Jack did not participate in this segment of the conversation. Katie, Cherie, Maryellen were all dancing to this weird song by the Broken Bells, "The High Road". It is kinda slow, so they looked like skinny trees in a mixed wind.

One confab that was private took place beside the grill. Jack was the meat minder and as he was turning the steaks over for the first time, Renfroe sidled up as if he didn't want to be seen by anyone. "Uh, Jack, I have a major transgression to offer up. Earlier tonight Ruby baited me like I was a moose in rut. Her quest was finding out the dirty details on your visiting Maryellen for an extended period of time last

Saturday. I folded like an envelope flap and told her the basic purpose of your visitation. This is my first violation of the kayak compact."

Jack finished the meat maneuvers and faced Renfroe. "All men have a weak spot. I guess we found yours, but thank you for telling me." Jack kept looking at his watch and Renfroe's big confession was totally ignored like it never happened. Renfroe thought to himself, something is wrong with Jack.

Jack turned and said, "I have to go in and make an announcement."

The dancing had discontinued and the music melded with the conversational buzz. Jack walked in, took his cooking fork and lightly tapped it against his beer bottle for attention. "My friends I would request your attention at this time. Five of you are our closest and best friends and one more of you has potential. Katie and I would like to make you aware of two changes in our life." Katie walked over and took Jack's hand and he continued, "On Wednesday of last week, we discovered that we had a *here to fore* unknown family. We have a daughter and a granddaughter, Kasein and Kalia Russell. When I went home that night Katie said the following to me.

"Jack, we are getting married tomorrow. I cannot be a grandmother unless we are married. Call Renfroe in the morning and set it up for 3:00 tomorrow afternoon."

Jack with a magnificent smile on his face and a voice that crumbled just slightly, "Katie and I are now man and wife forever." Katie who had moved to his side held up her ringed finger and gave Jack one of those short kisses. A short kiss that carried the weight of forever. Applause all around but blank looks were in abundance as the announcement sunk in.

Right on cue the doorbell rang. Katie, opened the door to Kasein and Kalia standing in the opening with anticipatory looks on each face. "Come in and meet our friends."

Cherie was the first to swoop down on the girls. "I am Cherie and this is my man, Trip.

She was followed closely by Ruby and Renfroe. Questions flew at them like birds in a flock.

Maryellen, seemed to be talking to herself. She had that revolving door sensation; the openings were going by too fast for her. Happy for

Katie and Jack, but she could not dismiss the consternation that rolled through her like rapids in a river. She felt as if drama was being pulled out of her like weeds in a flower bed. Her relationship with Katie won out and she went over to the door gathering.

The girls assumed the positions of daughter for the entire group. Kasein said later that it was like being under a waterfall, but a good waterfall. They were quickly family. After a little while, Kalia was taken to the guest room by her new grandmother and went to sleep. Kasein was soon the butt of jokes, a dealer of sarcasm cards and generally treated as a permanent fixture.

Jack just smiled the night away.

The party coasted to a slow resolve and all went home... happy for the time being.

BACK AND FORTH

KATIE SPREAD OUT ON her bed, while Jack did his nightly migration outside to pee on the grass. She and Maryellen had talked while everyone was playing cornhole, so their conversations were between just the two of them. The words, "I'm sorry", came out of their mouths like synchronized swimmers, and they both laughed. Immediately they reentered the buddy cove they had missed for so long. Katie smiled and knew she was a mother and grandmother. The night had been a good night on all fronts.

Maryellen sat and looked out her window and thought of the kiss she had just experienced with Tolliver. It was good and she was glad she had not rammed him with her nose. Had she done that Tolliver would have thought he had kissed a chicken. He was good guy, but who knew which path they would take or how long it would last. She was still nervous, but less so.

Jack was still peeing on the grass and looking at the stars. He knew people thought him irreligious or some form of non- believer. But, providing urine to kill weeds, having great admiration for sky toys and finding out he had a family gave him this tidbit of insight, that he wasn't just deposited here with the significance of a one dollar bill in an offering plate. Then he remembered that during the party, he and Maryellen were sharing the task of dish washing. While washing the knives and forks, she without looking at him said just two words. "Lunch tomorrow."

Kasein lay in the dark and felt like she was glowing and warm. She knew she had done good. Kalia rolled over and asked, "Mommy, where are we?"

"Baby, we are in your grandfather and grandmother's house."

Kalia rolled over and said "Good."

BIG SATURDAY

KATIE SLOWLY LET THE light gather in her eyes without raising her head from her pillow. The remains of the tequila had not yet been cremated. Her first thoughts were, damn, I have to get up and clean the kitchen. But this thought kick started the anamnesis of Jack and Maryellen at the sink with their backs to everyone. What was said? Was anything said? She had to admit that she had watched them all night like a seasoned gumshoe. Not one glance between them, total attention to Tolleson by Maryellen. What was the game? If there was a game, what were the rules?

Katie quickly closed that thought door and went to another area. What was Kalia going to call her. It could not be one of those grandmother non-bon mots like meemaw or grannie. She wanted to be called Katie. She made a mental note to address that issue at breakfast.

Maryellen wandered through her house as if walking through a maze. She definitely did not know where she was going. Her decision midway through last night's soiree was still strange to her. What was the provenance of her actions? Discombobulation reigned supreme. Jack is going to show up and I am going to …Do what?

If last night was a novel I was writing, would I put the backspace key to good use and eliminate those two words. Did I just want to get laid? Was it just that, if so, why not Tolliver? She knew the answer to that question, it was too soon for Tolliver, he has potential for a long term contract.

All of sudden it came clear to her she did want to get laid and Jack could provide that conjugation. Of course, he would be acting strictly within the protocol guidelines of a technician in a biology research lab.

Jack was pushing himself back from the table at the waffle house. The words, *Lunch Tomorrow*, bounced around in his head like a loose football. He had departed his home early, leaving a note. Kasein and Kalia were still asleep.

Katie was going to do the mani/pedi thing with Kasein and Kalia, which caused her to think of Jack and one of his harebrained ideas to open one of those places just for men and call it Toe Job. As per usual nothing got past the "thinking about it" stage and that's a good thing.

Jack knew he was going to Maryellen's. Any anguish went straight to the ashcan. He could not dance around this issue any longer.

Slowly the evening events replayed themselves through Katie's mind and another event took its place in the feature reprise. Katie unraveled the small meeting in the kitchen that had taken place as the party was on its last legs. She, Cherie, Trip, Ruby and Kasein were the only attendees. The floor leaders were Katie and Cherie. Their words flew back and forth like a shuttlecock over a badminton net.

Sometimes when those two got together it was like the parliament of Great Britain, interruptions of each other were part of the game. Conversational etiquette was in absentia. Ruby, Trip and Kasein were like fans at a tennis match. Keeping up with the subject matter would have required an official scorer.

Just when both combatants paused to catch their breath. Trip ventured onto the court and said, "Cherie and I are getting married." Ruby being the only other one, besides Trip, not getting her chin dirty on the floor, spoke appropriately and asked at the same time. "Congratulations and when?"

Cherie stood close to Trip with her head gently rested on the big guy's shoulder. "Well," she said "Until this man-o-mine transmogrified into a blabber face, it was a secret between just him and me. Yes, we are going to repeat the marital vows one month and one day from now. You are all invited and if possible, could we contain this news from everyone else until next weekend when there will be a formal declaration. I guess with the announcements earlier in the evening, Mr. Trip thought this was an appropriate time. I agree."

As Katie returned to the present, she quickly picked up the phone and dialed Cherie, a hoarse male voice said, "Good Morning. This is Trip the Intended on this end. To whom am I speaking? My first guess is Katie. Do I win a prize?"

"Yes, Trip, it is Katie. May I speak to your intended."

Another hoarse voice answered, "Yes, this is the fiancée of record, Cherie. Yes, I am going to wear a white dress. Yes, you are going to be in the wedding. Yes, it will be an open bar. Yes, we will have good music. What else?"

Katie, said, "Brunch at Schooners. 11:00. That good with you?"

"Good with me," was the answer.

Eleven o'clock at Schooners, a waterside restaurant that had called itself a local kind of place for decades. That was only partially true, as the tourists, being the nosy bunch that they are, found it to be good place to go. The music was always good, food above average, and you could wear anything you wanted, as long as the privates were kept private. Katie in her usual relaxed stroll sashayed through the large entrance room. Several sets of male eyeballs trailed her across the floor. She was sixty-five but it was sexy sixty-five.

She found Cherie already cubbied up to a tall drink with pieces of orange and pineapple straddling the rim of her glass. The weather was clear and mild and the gulf slick as a baby's ass. Katie slid into her seat as if she was a glaze.

"Alright, Cherie, this is the rule. I get to talk for as long as I want. You are only allowed to answer questions and the answers should be sheparded within the interrogatory proposed. No sidestepping."

Katie opened with, "Why... Is the question that is the headline of this morning's edition. All other questions are destined for the society page."

Cherie bore the look of a student that was well prepared for the test. "There is not one answer for that question, 'Why' might be a three-letter word but it covers a lot of personal turf. So, I will have to expand my answer to satisfy the question. I am fifty years old and have never been married. Until now there has not been one relationship that put me to bed at night with surety that it would see the sunrise in the morning. At this point in my life, being with Trip is like being a trapeze artist with a perpetual safety net. He is always there, maybe with a dip in his lip, a goofy smile on his face, but he is there and has my back in any and all situations. I love Trip with the strength of my entire being. If you besmirched him in any way, I can truthfully say, our friendship might be ripped asunder or at least put in timeout.

"I am one hundred percent aware of his faults. He snores. He loves his dog just a little too much. He has children by a previous mismarriage. But in a boxing match, the positives would win by a knockout in the first round. He loves sex. He can cook and I can't. He runs his business with energy and integrity, and he says my little tits taste like chocolate chip cookies.

"We enjoy a lot of the same things, music, food, drinking beer, playing cornhole, hunting and fishing. And the things we don't share or we disagree on, we just ignore. We keep our respective asses out of those conflicts and put them under the 'don't matter' door mat. That should just about do it, but I am open to more specific interrogation."

Katie for once had a relatively short answer. "Well, I guess that takes care of that. I guess we start getting ready for the big event."

Katie, looked at her freshly delivered drink, moved the pineapple and lemon slices around. She raised her head and retook the reins of the conversation.

"Now to make a u-turn back to me. I have to bare my soul at this point and come clean that I did not come here to talk about your conjoining as the single subject.

"I was going to advance a two-pronged agenda. The second prong has to do with my Proposition that is starting to look as ugly as guts. I feel as if I made two major miscalculations. I projected my proboscis into someone else's life path."

Katie pushed her case forward with the following, "Maryellen was consumed by sorrow, but I should have stood aside and let that tide ebb as a natural course for Maryellen as it seems to be doing at the present.

"The second mistake goes like this. I was way out of my weight class in thinking that I had the ability to insert the genuine love of my life into a situation that would require my understanding his sleeping with another woman, even if it was my best friend. I might add that this was done without his permission. If there was a Nobel Prize for stupidity, I should win for several years, as I feel that I have possibly done permanent damage to my relationship with Jack. We might still be together but in my mind, it would be like when someone is in a wreck and loses a partial leg. They can still walk, but not near as well as before the amputation. I feel as if I am made of small sticks.

"Maryellen and I have been grand friends with a relationship that has bridged a ton of tragedies. Minis and big ones. Never once have we not been there, never once was there a shimmer of distrust or lack of loyalty. I have done something that could cause a permanent crack in that sisterhood.

"A person is lucky in life to have one love of their life and even luckier to also have been blessed with a lifetime friend. I was one of the luckier ones in that I had both and it was wonderful to have that foundation everyday. I knew that no matter what, they had my back and would love me no matter what. I was conceited enough to think that I could heal someone with my dipstick diagnosis that has caused a personal dystopia."

The silence coagulated over the table like a big scab. Nobody said anything. Cherie took what a man might call a swig from her glass and said, "I think we should order some food. I am going to have a grouper sandwich. What about you?"

Katie, boosted the word 'perplexed' to another level with the look on her face. "Is that all you have to say? Order some food."

Cherie parried that thrust with a prepared smile. "Well missy, if you will replay your selfie sermon, you will discover that you said it all. Your answers are floating there like seaweed in the ocean. You did not bring me here to tell you everything would be fine and dandy. You brought me here to listen to you parade your wrong headedness around this table. If you will remember when you first revealed your Proposition, my one concern was that it would destroy the duo of you and Maryellen. I said you should not go forward with this risky business if it exposed your relationship to radiation. You cannot let that happen. If you want to once again enjoy the love of two people who love you like none other... Call a meeting and throw yourself on the floor and scream mea culpa. That's your best bet. They still love you. You just took a dish of vanilla ice cream and poured vinegar in it."

At that exact moment, a knuckle was knocking on a door and the door was answered by Maryellen and she said, "Hello Jack. Would you like a drink. I have made us chicken sandwiches with fresh lettuce and slices of cucumber as thin as paper."

Jack's first inclination was to run like hell, but that thought did not pass muster. The next thing he knew, Maryellen took him by the hand and led him into the kitchen area. The small table was set and ready. He felt like everything was set and ready, except for himself. He slowly eased into the waiting chair. Not a word escaped from his mouth. He felt like the kid in class who had been asked a question with no answer anywhere to be found.

Maryellen sat across the table from him and just looked. Jack thought she was going to poke him with her finger like she was buying an avocado... But she didn't. She spoke very softly as if they were at a cocktail party and she wanted just one more drink. "Jack, this is the turnback session. You can leave the sandwich uneaten and walk out the door or you can stay. I have spent a blue ton of time on this decision and I have arrived at the conclusion that I need a sex shove. I have a friend now that has possibilities, but I am afraid that old axiom about riding a bicycle might not be applicable to a sixty-five-year-old female, who has entered the world of re-virginity. I need to slip back into the sack at least once to test out the equipment. Jack, you and I are friends. Not lovers, we will never be lovers. You love Katie, I shall always love Enos. Friends sometime do things for their friends that they might not do for others. I want to have sex with you and I want to do it today. This will be the only time that we do the deed. There will be no repechage in this relationship. As far as I am concerned the memory will be buried like an ancient Egyptian. I would like to think of us sometime in the future attending a backyard barbeque with a beer in one hand and our lover's hand in the other. We would be talking about the unusual weather of the season. Awkwardness, anxiety, and apprehension would not be part of the portrait. I would describe it as a bagatelle. Conversation flowing like we all were in a small easy whirlpool."

Jack sat like the proverbial bump on a log, but he talked. "Maryellen, do you know the term "j'etoube?" I am going to take that blank face as a negative. J'etoube is what one chess player says to his opponent when he wants to touch one of his pieces to just adjust it, not to make a move. From your previous oration I think you are saying to me, J'toube."

Jack continued, "Maryellen, there are few times in my life that I can say I honestly made love. The great majority of those were during the past year or so. What I am saying is that I am familiar with the exercise you described. I might add that I cannot bring to mind anytime that I have had it described as more or less a contractual contrivance. Since we are making each other aware of exactly our positions on this groundbreaking event, you must remember you are dealing with a contractor that has unreliable tools. Sometimes they work well, sometimes they relax a little too much and sometimes they just say "fuck it", of course I mean in a figurative sense. You have said your piece and I have said mine. Do you have any addendums to the bylaws or should we just adjourn this meeting without further discussion? After we eat these sandwiches of course."

Until that very second, Jack had not noticed what Maryellen was wearing. She had on a pair of black well fitted pants and a gray cashmere long sleeved sweater. She was barefooted and the 'girls' hung undisciplined. Jack spoke around a bite of sandwich, "Maryellen, we have created an atmosphere conducive to a board of directors meeting, not a sexual adventure. So as the first order of lessening the scholarly stiffness that abounds in this room, would you lean over and give me a flicker of a kiss."

Which she did. She left a glisten of a taste between lemon and orange and she smiled like the cat that was anticipating the mouse. The sandwiches were done. Maryellen, pointed towards a bottle of rum and asked if he would like a drink. Jack thought, I don't want a drink. I need a drink. He nodded his consent. The drinks were poured.

The next move was into the living room. There was music, Ashley Monroe singing "Hands on You." Jack thought, now that's a major icebreaker. It must have worked. They were quickly dancing in the darkened room. Talking took a hike and things progressed as if on a well-marked pathway. Hands moved from one soft place to the next, kisses lasted a little longer and eyes fluttered like butterfly wings. They entered that space where stop signs did not exist, and they continued to slowly undulate with the music. Jack kissed her ear and whispered, "You smell delicious," and slowly eased the sweater over her head and it fell out of his hand like a small cloud. The pants slid down like they were tired of being around her waist and she stepped out of them as if it was a natural order. The pants lay where they were abandoned like two black ropes. She quivered, looked at Jack and said, "Don't leave me hanging," and he didn't. Clothes were everywhere except on bodies. They looked at each other and both started laughing.

"Why don't we repair to the boudoir, my lady." They did and the clothes were left all alone.

The laughs touched the brakes just a little as they entered the room. No lights but the sun sent shards of light into the room which spread across the already turned down sheets. The two naked bodies stood facing the bed and Jack whispered, "Maryellen, if we are going to do this and make it a solitaire occasion, let's slow down, go get the music, our drinks and we could create a cuddle huddle to decide which play we want to run."

Maryellen, released a held breath that she had been holding like a new found treasure and said, "I agree."

When she returned Jack was laying on the near side of the bed, he moved to the other side and held the sheet open for her. He left his arm underneath her pillow, so that when she slipped into the bed, her head was cradled inside his arm and they were both looking straight up at the ceiling.

They lay on the bed and sunlight still poked its head through the curtains and lay across their bodies like swaddling clothes. Music by different folk came and went and their heads soon faced each other. Nothing touched... at first... Jack and Maryellen talked about Katie and Enos as if they were people they had known a long time ago. Jack touched Maryellen like she was hot water and he just wanted to test the heat. Maryellen trembled and she touched Jack with a hand that was eager but scared. Jack took his right hand and rolled Maryellen over on her stomach and began to caress her lower back with a practiced stroke. This continued over the entire territory and ended with his kissing the back of her knees while his hand lightly caressed her derriere as if it had a different agenda. He slid up her body until he covered her completely, with one hand he lifted the hair off her neck and kissed a small spot just above her shoulders. That kiss started as a light touch but gathered intensity until it could be described as a force. He then rolled her over onto her back and they kissed with gentleness which masked the mounting arousal. The kiss had long legs and they entered another level of intensity. The intensity map showed that their destination would soon be reached.

With her free hand she touched Jack's shoulder and with a tiny push she rolled him over on his back. In a synchronized move with her body she straddled Jack and their body parts were matched as planned since the beginning of time. She pushed herself up with her arms and looked at Jack and said in a voice of conviction. "Do it Jack, do it now," and took him in her hand to make the joining.

Like a spasm, Jack felt a certain weakness flow through his body like icy water. It was a cousin to a small electric shock. Maryellen shuddered as if chilled and not from excitement. These actions were simultaneous. For both of them it was like when a night watchman goes through a building and turns the lights off from one room to the next. Maryellen and Jack looked at each other and smiled. Maryellen said in a very controlled whisper, "We just couldn't do it, could we?"

Jack nodded his head, "The line was too bright to cross."

"Jack, I will love you forever for this. I think you showed me that the gate would open when the right person turned the lock. What do you think we should tell Katie? I say we don't tell her anything. She still stands in the penalty box for starting this...Let her think whatever she wants."

"Maryellen, how about a cup of coffee and let's play rock paper scissors to see who goes and get the clothes." Maryellen offered to go get the clothes, but told Jack he couldn't look.

Later while finishing up the coffee and munching on a lemon drop cookie, they laughed together like two people who had just escaped a horrible death. Jack asked, "What was that scent you had on, it was intoxicating?"

Maryellen, with a guilty smile, answered. "It is ylang-ylang, supposed to be an aphrodisiac."

Jack laughed and said, "I had a friend in college who was not to bright. He thought an aphrodisiac was a black man's hairdo."

They both agreed that it was great fun and how they both were into it big time, but there came a time when the fire was quenched. It was like their bodies had a governor that just allowed a certain speed and nothing more. Jack leaned over Maryellen, took her hand like it was a grand gift and gave her a kiss that was considered by both to be a goodbye. Their hands drifted apart after a small squeeze from both directions.

KATIE REPAIRS

KATIE LEFT THE PARKING lot of Schooners with a determined countenance... A reflection of her brunch with Cherie. Her singular thought was of Jack. She had once read a book where the female described her lover as the last piece of her puzzle. Katie rolled that thought around a little and came to the conclusion that a piece of a puzzle was not enough for her. A piece of the puzzle was not any different from the others and they all were equally important. She thought of Jack as the last line of her poem. The last ray of a poem was in her case the line that pulled it all together and was more important than any others. Yes, Jack was the last gathering of her life poem. She thought of the last line in a poem by Herman Hesse, "When I Go to Sleep". It ended with, "Where the gathering of souls commences."

This poem was one of four that were used by Richard Strauss for his final song series, "The Last Four Songs." Ironically, Jack loved to listen to those songs, although he had no idea what they were singing. Even worse, for many years, whenever speaking about them, he would use Johann Strauss, not Richard Strauss as the composer. But, as Jack said, "They are brothers and that is close enough." That last line would also be significant to Maryellen as she carries in her soul the belief that she and Enos will be reunited, as did he. Katie opened the unlocked door in her mind that led to the Maryellen world.

Cherie had told her what to do about her dilemma, but she only confirmed what Katie had known for several days. She hated to use the phrase "man up," but that is what she was going to have to do.

She had no intention of spending the last remaining coins in her life pocket without hearing Maryellen say, "just for shits and giggles, lets buy a new bra," or watch her mentally trample over some nouveau intellect in her library. Katie remembered the middle-aged harlequin who proclaimed that she had an IQ of 153, which was supposed to go along with her oversized butt and hands that shook like frightened leaves. Maryellen destroyed her like a paper doll and left her distraught at the library counter and blubbering that no one understood her. Maryellen's final comment was, "If you would like to pay your overdue charges, we can break a hundred."

Katie knew she had exposed her two folk, who were the weight bearing walls in her life, to extreme fermentation by her stupidity. Katie drove on but noticed that she was driving slower and slower, just like she did when she used to partake of the occasional joint. In her mind, she decided she was trying to push the phone call she had to make just a little bit further down on her to do list. Suck it up. At sixty-five there are far more painful things than a super deluxe apology to your best buddy.

Katie picked up her phone, dialed three numbers and she heard a car door shut. It had to be Jack. He came in the front door with a beer in his hand. She said, "I see you have been drinking and driving again."

"Well yes, yes I have and I don't feel one pinprick of guilt," emoted Jack. "Have you talked with Kasein this am. I wonder how the party went with her?"

Katie answered the question before pushing forward with her real concern. "She and Kalia slept in a little. The first thing they wanted to know, was where you were. I explained to them that Saturday mornings you usually went to Waffle House and ate breakfast, read the paper, sometimes read a book. I told them you would be back soon. They had to leave, Kalia had a meeting with her new soccer team. This is her first season. Also, Kasein felt a little out of sorts this am, as did I."

Jack wore a genuine look of disappointment on his face. Katie could tell he was thinking, I have a lot to learn about this grandfather deal.

Katie turned the conversation back to her original concern like a race driver making a sharp corner.

Katie asked herself the question, you might not feel any guilt about drinking beer and driving, but do you feel guilty for your participation in casual carnality? Then she asked out loud, "Where have you been all morning?"

Jack looked totally prepared for the inquisition, "I have been eating chicken sandwiches with lettuce and thinly sliced cucumber pieces. Those delicacies were followed by some rum concoction that I did not recognize. Oh yeah, I went by to see Renfroe, but he was gone to see his granddaughter. They are going to North Carolina tomorrow. He goes there all the time. Sometimes I wish he had never bought that house up there. I also went to get a haircut, but the wait was too long. As I walked back to my car there was a guy sitting on the sidewalk playing a guitar. Not bad. He played some John Prine songs which don't require much voice. I stood there for a while and I thought about what I was doing. I was basking in the busking." He followed this with a guttural chuckle and a faint smile lightly painted on his face. He was enjoying this, so he pushed his gloat chips all in to the middle of the table. "What you been doing?" in his best Joey Tribbiani voice.

This was the opportunity for her to assume the prostrate position, but she avoided it like a point guard with a killer crossover dribble.

Her excuse to herself was that Maryellen should get the first handful of repentance. Right or wrong, who knows. She answered with a scrap of perkiness that just did not fit the occasion. "I met Cherie at Schooners for brunch. We had a great time, solved a couple of the global glitches now in play. I have to call the President with our solutions. Mainly, we talked about her upcoming conjugal connection. She seems to be as happy as I have ever seen her. It is going to be, as she described it, a gigantic galactic goose gaggle. I am going to be a mature replication of a maid of honor."

Jack moved toward the television. There had to be some sports event on that he could tolerate.

Katie just stood there with the telephone in her hand, then went into the backyard and sat in one of the outside chairs. Then finished what she had started earlier and called Maryellen.

MARYELLEN
RIDES A BIKE

MARYELLEN WAS SITTING IN her kitchen, waiting...She had gotten the flash that she needed to be near her phone. Something was coming her way and she could not miss it. The ringer on her phone broke the silence like a rude child.

Maryellen had practiced her hello to be the consummate casual greeting. She had a friend, Amy, who had the best hello. She lived in Ohio and whenever you called Amy she would answer "Hel", drop three notes, "Lo." She gave it her best effort as she wanted to answer Katie in that fashion...Hello, and the answer came.

"Hey Maryellen, this is Tolliver, what are you doing?"

She gathered herself and answered "Nothing much, what about you?"

He answered, "I have been puttering around all day and I have to say that is the first time I have ever described my actions as puttering. I think it means I haven't done anything of consequence. What I have done is basically nothing. I thought of you as someone who would know something, I could do that would allow me to remove the entry of 'putterer' from my resume."

Maryellen, did not hesitate one split second, "Do you have hiking boots? If so, put them on and give me about half an hour to make us some chicken sandwiches and you can stop on the way over here and pick up a good bottle of chardonnay." Maryellen chuckled a low laugh as she pinned the title of semi-slut on herself... That had to be right. I am using the same chicken as sustenance for two men as I knock on the entrance to the halls of mature promiscuity.

As Maryellen hit the discontinue button on her phone, it vibrated with another call. She did not slow down to give the big hello. She just knew it was Katie this time and she did not want to talk long.

"Maryellen, this is your lost friend, Katie. Could we talk soon? I cannot go one more day without you in my life. Please come to my house for breakfast in the morning. Just show up when you want."

Maryellen just stood there like a glass figurine. Sometimes stressful moments pile up like bricks and the weight of the accumulation breaks out emotions that had lain dormant for a long time. Maryellen muttered, sotto voce, "I would like that also. See you at nine in the morning." Tiny tears crept out of the corner of her eyes, but she was smiling like a person cleansed of anguish.

Toliver arrived at her front door properly attired as per the directions from Maryellen. The first words out of his mouth were, "Do you mind if I ask where we're going?"

She answered, "I don't mind one iota. There is a hiking trail that goes around the entire state of Florida. We just so happen to have a portion of it about twenty-five miles north of here. I thought we might hike two miles down the trail to a swinging bridge over the creek, have mid afternoon tea, sans tea, and return back. It is not a highly sanitized trail, but also not uncomfortable…You up for it?"

After two wrong turns and not much conversation of relevance, they arrived at the trailhead and parked the car. Soon all the carry along stuff was out of the car. Toliver had a black backpack that looked like it had been put to good use while he was in the Navy. He had been very quiet about his military experience. The entire description to this point had been, "I was in the Navy until I retired."

Maryellen led off down the path. Blackberry bushes guarded the left side of the trail for a while but gave up their watch to scrub oaks and pines for the rest of the hike. Some up, some down but the net direction was down until the trail mimicked the turns of the creek as if they were chasing each other. There was not much conversation, and it was only about the trail. Maryellen and Toliver took their time and soon they approached the swinging bridge. It looked like it was taken from a movie set. They crossed the bridge and Toliver revealed the contents of his pack, to include a small blanket, bottle of wine and a tiny Bluetooth speaker. Maryellen had the chicken salad sandwiches in a small fanny pack. They sat and listened to the water sounds from the creek as they created a contrapuntal mosaic with the peace and quiet that dressed them from top to bottom.

Toliver took the mic first and said, "Maryellen, I've been watching you from behind all the way here. You have a terrific tush and it preoccupied my attention for a good amount of the way. I actually tripped over roots a couple of times, but the prevalent condition that I observed today for you is a one-worder: Pensive. It's like you participated in an act of sanctification but don't know if you are fully consecrated. That might be a poor analogy but it's the best I can come up with at the present. How about a glass of wine?"

Maryellen, accepted the wine and looked at Toliver as if he was a channeler. She would have to think about the analogy that he just used, but she grasped the gist of it... At the same time, she made a decision to put her thoughts on the blanket. "Toliver, you and I have been together just a few times, but I am going to assert that we have a connection that is a shared kinship. Maybe at eighteen you don't say these things but being sixty- five shortens your time horizons and causes you to push the envelope a little bit faster in order not to waste even one day of something good. I am placing a wager that you feel the same way. So here goes, and if at any time you want to get up and run to the car, please call Katie and tell her where I am. She will come and get me."

Toliver dropped his head for a second as if he was going to pray, "Maryellen, I have participated in a very good life and was lucky enough to share it with someone who I loved with great intensity and was loved equally in return. I miss her every day but even more I miss the convection of energy, respect and honesty that we shared. I think that you and I share this remembrance of things past and revere their existence. We have come to realize that the existence of those thoughts creates a sorrow that cannot be put aside by oneself. I have known from the coffee shop that we were at least friends. And if I was lucky, I might get lucky... So, go on and make your bet."

Maryellen was laying back with her hands behind her head, Toliver was sitting in that yoga position with your legs crossed, which was strange for a man of his size. Maryellen, without saying a word, sat up and sat the same way directly in front of Toliver. With their knees almost touching, she looked directly at him like a camera lens. "I remember Enos like it was yesterday. I remember all the little things," like what his hands looked like, the black dot on his left arm from being stuck with a pencil by the preacher's daughter in the sixth grade. The look on his face as he tried to get his tie straight in the morning. I also remember the big things and the unnatural kindness that permeated our song of life. We were an unmatched duet. You are right in your summation that those musings can push you into a dark corner of life's big room. I'm rattling on when I should tell you what I intended.

"My best friend, Katie, recognized this long before I did. Her solution was to loan Jack to me as a retrieval device from sitting atop the cairn I carefully constructed each and every day. Long story short, Jack and I never consummated the Proposition. That is what we named it. It did let me discover that I could be a participant in the life of love and swim in the deep water of affection and endearment. I will spare you the minutiae of the Jack being Maryellen's penultimate prom date. We realized that we were ill-used puppets, that were capable of cutting our strings. We walked away with a smile and both of us gained a friend for life.

"Unbeknownst to you," she continued with gathering confidence. "You had a few lines in this drama. I described you to myself as a player who had the potential to be in the lineup for a long time. Sooooooo, do you want to go to one of our houses and see if a consommé of consummation could be a proper end to this picnic?"

Toliver unfolded his legs from what looked like an untenable position and said these words without a glimpse of humor, "Will you be gentle with me?" And followed that with a little laugh that underscored his statement as genuine.

The hike back to the car was slow, as if they wanted to give the coming event as big a buildup as possible. Who knows what they were thinking? But anyone who might have passed them on the trail should have known that both had something else on their mind besides not tripping on a tree root.

When they got in the car, the conversation broke out like the measles. Apparently, both had been stowing thoughts, concerns and questions all the way up the trail. Tolliver went first. "Since we have adopted the cornerstones of our relationship to be honesty and openness, which, by the way I think it should be, you should know I have not done anything like this since Eve slipped away. I enjoy the way you talk about Enos and I hope I can do the same with Eve. There are parallels that could be used as ballast in a new relationship, or those same parallels could also be underlying currents of tension and distrust. I know I will always love Eve and I know you will always love Enos. I don't look at either one of us taking their places. I have come to believe those loves can be deemed a delineation for us not to accept any less from others in any shape, form or fashion. I will shut up now as the next phrase would probably be described as babble."

Maryellen looked at Toliver with a look of amusement and understanding. "Damn, I thought all this time you just wanted to get in my pants. You sly devil. You had me with that first cup of coffee in the rain. Sometimes a blessing arrives on your doorstep without warning. I think that we should consider our two-person congregation to be a fermata... That is a note of unspecified length of time. Speaking of time, could you drive a little bit faster."

They had reached the time of big decision. My house or yours. If a person had a split screen television into both of their brains, they would have two versions of the same movie. Both of them were contemplating the location of their sexual license renewal. Ironically, they both had reached the same conclusion, but had taken separate routes.

He wanted to go to his house because it would be a part of his new life and would not be an olio of his former life. She still thought of her house as the house she shared with Enos. She could not separate her past from her present at this time. Little things would be present that would discolor her thoughts. If she and Toliver were in the bedroom just sitting on the bed and talking or anything else together, it would aborn her doing the same thing so many times with Enos. She needed a clean blackboard to transcribe this event. So, from different geneses they arrived at the same decision.

She reached over and touched Toliver on the leg. "Toliver, let's go to your house." He shared a smile with her, nodded his head in assent, then breathed a quiet sigh of relief.

As they approached his house, the day was calling it quits. They held hands as they went up the steps and entered the front door. Maryellen had a recurrence of the same feeling of settlement she had enjoyed on her initial visit to the house. It wafted through her like an easy dream. Their actions were somewhere between "let's do this" and "why don't we have a glass of wine and not be in a rush?" But, momentum took over and before anyone said anything, they were climbing the stairs, still holding hands.

The upstairs bedroom was extremely large. It took up the entire second story of the house except for the bathroom. There were not many pictures. Actually, the walls were approaching bareness and that was just fine with Maryellen. She was glad that Tolliver had not created a Tolliver/Eve memorial. No lights were on and the day had taken a few more steps towards darkness. That was a good thing, as neither looked to be pawing the floor to get naked

Tolliver reached for her hand, then walked her over to a large chair and seated her. He then knelt down and removed her hiking boots and socks. Still no talking. He walked over to a speaker on a dresser and turned on soft music. He then sat in a chair directly across from her and removed his boots and socks. They sat and looked at each other as if assessing each other's barefootedness. As if on a signal, two quiet chuckles glided across the room and met in the middle. A filigree of emotion was created by the universal jeweler only for the two of them.

It was on after that.

They both read off the same script, as if this was the premier after many rehearsals. After the final act was done and the curtain came down, there was silence. Then applause sprinkled from different spots and then thunderous noise, to include tiny shouts of bravo.

Maryellen lay on her back and released a small smile intended only for her enjoyment. She was a happy girl. Tolliver had the composure of an artisan who was pleased and surprised by his handiwork. He also lay on his back with both hands behind his head, as if replaying the event just to make sure it was real. There had been laughs of joy and abandonment throughout, the copula chitchat had been sparse but on point. They both lay there as if allowing time to implant them with a permanent memory.

Tolliver rolled over to look at Maryellen and she returned the favor. She said, "I think it will take a good hard scrubbing to get that smile off your face."

He answered, "Yes it will, but does this mean I can call you my girlfriend?"

She said, "At this point, I think we should not go to public outcry. Not yet, but soon." Then as if hesitant to speak, she said, "I think Enos and Eve would be happy for us."

Then Maryellen said, "I'm hungry."

Tolliver said "Well then, let's eat something." Both laughed and Tolliver added, "You stay here and I'll bring it up, but you have to stay naked."

Kalia was in her room reading her new Nancy Drew books. Kasein still felt as if she was wearing a heavy coat. Something was akilter in her life and she did not know what. She just knew that a bad thing was in the making.

Tolliver returned quickly with a shallow crystal bowl filled with fruit and two flutes of champagne. "I anticipated that we might return here after the hike and I thought this would be a good thing to eat. It seems even more appropriate now."

Maryellen lay on her side with her hand propping up her head, "You should write in your diary that you have been spot on throughout the day, at least after you stopped puttering."

"While you were gathering up your fruit salad. I used the time to contemplate the blueprint we might follow for a while. I came up with a big blank piece of drafting paper. We have only been together four times. At this point, we know we both like music and food, and the sex works well. Being sixty- five dyes a new relationship with both hesitance and the lack thereof. I say we let the already established glide path to remain in place. In other words, we do what we think works, be honest and candid with each other. We both wear a vulnerable jacket, but this is offset by the following statement. I am judging both of us to be kind folk and hurtfulness is foreign to both of us." A brief silence ensued. "Boy, I thought a lot of stuff while you were gone."

Toliver kinda laughed and said, "Actually, my main concern was not to drop the salad bowl or spill the wine while walking up the stairs. You did say a lot, and it can be condensed into a smaller version I see us as lucky that we have discovered someone in a similar life juncture. We both understand the straits put upon us by death. In my opinion we will at least come out the other end of this shindig with a very good friend and at the most with the second chapter of romance in our life. Let's let this water reach its own level and both of us partake of it as a thirsty soul."

After the fruit disappeared and the wine was drunk, a duvet of awareness covered both with a need for clothes. It was funny to both of them that they felt this at the same time. This question leapt into the middle of the bed. "What do we do now?"

That interrogative would not have been necessary decades ago. They would have just done it again... probably better than the first time. But, not having that option begs that question, what do we do now?

Food is always a good answer, so that is what they did. Tolliver cooked two fine hamburgers with a baked potato. The discourse jumped from subject to subject during the meal and afterwards they sat in the living room and listened to music and talked about books.

Until Maryellen christened a new topic. "Tolliver, this has been a great entry into a venery circus, but now I had better go home. Today has been lovely and perfect. Do you remember what you said to me the first day we met at the library? When we parted you said 'a demain' and I replied not tomorrow but soon. Tonight, I am going to say 'a demain' to you and expect you to say, maybe tomorrow and surely soon."

The ride home was silent. There was a brief kiss, she remained at the door until he entered his car, then she gave him a wave goodbye.

GOOD AND BAD

KATIE WAS ABOVE THE covers as her mind helicoptered from Jack to Maryellen to Enos and back and forth and back and forth. Sleep was a distant drum for her tonight. She had wanted to be right but she had missed the target by a bunch.

Jack had a Katie meter that worked wonders. He just knew when to stay in the living room and watch whatever. His confidence level as the owner of this feelometer had suffered major damage since Katie had dropped the Proposition bomb. Tonight, it issued a strong stayaway signal and he did. He did not feel well himself for some reason. He could not put his finger on it, but there was a cockroach consciousness crawling in his chest. He remembered the words of warning by the doc, he wondered if his body was sending him semaphore signals of distress or if it was that familiar villain, too much stress?

Sometime around 11:30 a semi naked woman sat in his asleep lap and whispered in his ear. "Baby, come to bed. I miss you." All's well that ends well... sometimes.

It's two thirty in the morning and two ladies conjoined at the heart stared at their respective ceilings and their thoughts spiraled into the air and solved not one thing. One of them thought, "What will I say to her?" and the other was a perfect fit. "What will she say to me?" Then they would switch off to and fro. As usual, thoughts at this time of the night brought no answers to either question.

SUNDAY SAD SUNDAY

SUNDAY MORNING WAS INTRODUCED to its audience with a cold rain that felt like needle points, thunder like a bass drum line, wind that burned and lightning that caused a person to run inside.

Jack got up early, dressed, gave the sleeping Katie a dot of a kiss. He left her a note, that said, "I know you are having breakfast with Maryellen. Remember you told me last night. I have that feeling that you would prefer this not being a two on one fast break. I will get breakfast and see you later. Call me when she leaves."

Katie eased out of the bed and as was her usual practice, all occasions required the proper attire. She decided on black jeans, black sandals, peach colored tee shirt, hair pulled back and tied with strip of cloth that matched the tee-shirt.

Maryellen thought to herself. I have missed Katie more than I realized Three months ago, I would have called her on the phone earlier this evening and might have even gone over to her house. She needs to know that I am a dues paying member of the loved and the loving once again. I shall wear bright colors as if I were in a parade. She wore pale yellow slacks, dark blue long-sleeved shirt that had a small collar. As a final statement, she wore a bright red raincoat. She felt fine, started to call Toliver, but didn't.

Jack drove slowly in the rain as he ruminated. He hesitated as a purl of pain slithered across his chest, which he dismissed out of hand. He tried to create the scene at his house and said a short invocation for peace to reign supreme. Then he turned into the Waffle House parking lot and had a strange, out of place thought, 'There could be no finer last meal than two eggs over easy, crisp bacon, crisp hash browns, a crisp waffle and the eternal elixir, hot coffee. Eating breakfast alone with a good book was a grand way to enter the morning. He was reading a book of short stories by Thomas McGuane, recommended to him by that new guyfriend of Maryellen's. They discovered their mutual admiration for Larry McMurtry and the aforementioned Thomas McGuane.

As per usual, Maryellen came through the back door minus the knock. Katie was standing in the kitchen holding a cup of coffee, which she quickly left on the countertop. There were no words passed. They just walked not quite slowly, with arms outstretched and they embraced each other. They went far beyond a normal hug. This one had wings. They clung to each other as only family can do when someone who was lost, is found. If smiles were marketable, money would have been no object. At last they parted, sat on the couch, held hands and smiled again. Words at this point would only have been odd noise. They knew that the friendship had been restored to its former glory.

Jack drove on through the companion rain, he went past the house he used to live in, before Katie. Loneliness ran out the front door and got in the car with him. Solitary was an old companion of his during that tenure. Would he return to loneliness in death?

Damn, here it comes again. This time the purl had become a small wave and the pain had matured enough to give him a good punch in the chest. Something was wrong. He was dizzy and his vision had hidden behind a psychedelic patina. This was not good. He had trouble pulling the car over and tried to determine his location. The one thing he could see was a gigantic red arch and he knew where he was.

The pain had escalated to be a giant elephant foot on his chest. Could he hold his phone in his hand? He knew he was a short distance from Renfroe's house. His hand shook and the phone danced in his hand trying to get free, but he was able to get to his favorites and hit the Renfroe button.

Four rings later, a big Renfroe hello spilled out. Jack tried to talk but could not.... All he could say was, "Aaah, aah, Mc, Mc, Mc, don don".... On the other end Renfroe held the phone away from his head and looked at it and recognized the number was Jack. Jack was in trouble and the prior Wednesday skipped through Renfroe's mind. Renfroe held the phone up to his head again and heard the same disturbing mantra as before. Jack was at McDonalds; he ran to his car while hollering to Ruby. "Jack is in trouble. Call 911 and send an ambulance to the McDonalds downtown." And he ran out in the rain.

———— • • • ————

Katie was the first to speak. "The best advice I have garnered in a long time came yesterday from that soothsaying seer Cherie and if I were to take it in a literal fashion, I would be belly down on the floor and entreating you for mercy and grace. That action would get me all wrinkled and no one wants that and I know your parameters on idiotic behavior. So, I am going to go forward with my mea culpa and you can use your imagination on my prostration.

"Maryellen, I have been an ignoramus capable of combining my idiocy with being a pompous ass. For the last two days, I have been on a desperate search for one tiny twinkle of good in my proposition. There is none. Except maybe a lesson learned will improve my actions as I slink though the rest of my life. Please forgive me and may we put this in a place that it never sees another slice of light. Will you accept my apology?"

———— • • • ————

As for Jack, the small pain wave had grown into a tsunami and Jack went black.

Renfroe saw Jack's truck across the street from McDonalds. The best he could do was park cattywhompas with one wheel up on the curb and the back wheels out in the road. He slammed his car into park and ran to the truck. Jack was slumped over the steering wheel with his face turned to the window, his arms hung like old links of rope. His eyes were closed, but Renfroe thought he saw Jack gasp. There were no sounds other than the radio playing "Brown Eyed Handsome Man" by Van Morrison. Jack was no small person, but Renfroe picked him up out of the truck like he was a jockey and laid him on the pavement.

Later he remembered that the distant sound of a siren gave him hope. He started resuscitation on Jack as best he knew how.

The siren punctured his concentration and the ambulance skidded to a stop. Renfroe was whipped away by a large arm and came to rest on his butt in the wet street. In a scant minute, Jack was on a stretcher and they were gone.

Renfroe fumbled in his pocket for his telephone, then called the only person he considered capable of telling Katie. Ruby was running across the street in the rain and hugged Renfroe, he hung his head on her shoulder and cried.

Maryellen did not wait long to answer Katie's request. "Katie, you were wrong in your approach but correct in your purpose. It was difficult and at times I thought your love for Jack or I had been doused beyond doubt. But in the end, I could see what you wanted. Jack and I had great fun and by the way, his feet are not all that wonderful as you so described them. We nursed an awkward situation into a weaned friendship. Jack and I have confirmed that we could not do what was requested because we both could not cross that bright line. I am going to borrow a mathematical term. We were asymptotic We were limited in what we could do. We did make a few stabs at it, but the crossover could not occur. All of these occurrences might fall into a shenanigan category, but it forced me to accept my sorrow as something that could include an intimacy with someone else. My newly lit candle guided me out of the tunnel into the light. Bottom line, thank you. If you had not made such an ass of yourself, I might have been forlorn forever."

Hugs were in order. Katie and Maryellen just sat there, looking and smiling. Both had the single tear gliding down a cheek, but the world was back in balance once again.

The front door flew open and there stood Cherie. She walked into the room as if she could not make up her mind whether to run in or just walk fast. She seemed to be doing some kind of weird dance as she closed the distance between her and Katie. Cherie did not acknowledge the presence of Maryellen. "Katie, get your stuff. Jack is in the hospital and they think he had a heart attack. My car is outside, let's go."

In a millisecond, Katie went from smiling with tears, to a face as blank as a piece of new stationery. Katie went first to babbling unidentifiable sounds and then grabbed her control switch and start asking very logical questions. "Where is Jack? What did the doctors say? When did it happen? Where did it happen?"

Cherie said, "Let's get going and I'll tell you what I know."

The ride to the hospital was surprisingly quiet. Cherie answered all the basics. "Renfroe found him unconscious in his car across from the downtown McDonalds. Jack had called him from his truck. When he left his house, he told Ruby to call an ambulance. Renfroe was doing CPR on Jack when the ambulance got there. Jack never responded to anything the responders tried. The EMT people moved quickly and did all the usual things and took him to the emergency room, where they got him to come around in a very small way.

"They're pretty sure he had a heart attack, but not real sure on what kind. It happened about forty-five minutes ago. It is sketchy as to the time."

It was ironic to Katie that this should happen on Sunday morning. *Lots of people were either going in or out of the churches they passed... Dark suits, subdued dress colors, little girls dancing around like little girls do, teen agers looking like they had been released from severe oppression. Jack always thought of religion as a mirror in a fun house.*

Katie started fumbling around in her purse, looking for her phone. "I just remembered we have a family. I need to call Kasein."

Maryellen said, "Let me call, you have enough to cover now."

Katie quickly said, "No, they are my family. I should tell her."

The phone was dialed and quickly answered. "Hello"

Katie did not recognize the voice, "This is Katie, could I speak to Kasein?"

She could feel the eerie silence crawl inside of her like a cold water.

"This is Amelia her next door neighbor. You don't know do you? Kasein died this morning. She woke up and started to get Kalia out of bed and never made it out of her bedroom. Kalia came and got me, she was still alive. Her last words were for me to call Katie or Jack. Are you Katie?"

The phone dropped out of Katies hand as if she had been struck with a taser. Maryellen scrambled across the seat and picked up the phone. "Hello, hello, this is Maryellen, Katie's friend, what is going on? Katie can't talk, she is trying but nothing is coming out."

"I am Amelia, I live next door to Kasein, she died this morning. I am sorry, I am not thinking straight myself and I apologize for being so blunt. I just did not know what to do."

Maryellen answered back. "Let us call you back in a few minutes. We are on the way to the hospital. Jack had a heart attack this morning. We will call you back soon."

Katie felt despair descend on her like one of those heavy blankets they put on you when you have an x-ray, except this blanket covered her whole body. She sent Jack a message. *Be okay, please be okay. Please don't leave me now.*

Silence was the only question or answer for the rest of the trip.

Renfroe was standing outside the entrance as they slid into the parking lot. He spoke as if he was a guide in a museum, "He's in room 2371. He's still unconscious and is not responding to anything. The doctor is waiting to talk with Katie...Take the second elevator on the left."

Maryellen took over and stepped out of the car and spoke in her best librarian voice. "Renfroe, we just got word that Kasein died this morning. Her next door neighbor called. Katie cannot talk, she is almost catatonic. I know she wants to see Jack, but she also needs to know that Kalia is taken care of. As soon as you get us up to the room, it would be good for you to go over there and make sure the right things are done. Is Ruby here?

Renfroe answered, "She is upstairs waiting for all of us."

"I think it would be good for her to go with you, she has the most motherability skills in this group and a six-year-old little girl needs a Ruby. The neighbor's name is Amelia, she and Kasein are very close, so she should have all the info you might need." Renfroe snapped to like a private in the Marine Corps.

Katie was slumped over in the back seat like a broken doll. Renfroe opened the door and lifted her out of the car. The thought that he had lifted two bodies out of cars this morning flew through his mind like a rip saw. He whispered in Katie's ear. "Baby, you have to walk, Jack needs to see you. I will take care of Kasein and Kalia. You go see Jack."

A hesitant nod was all he got. He lowered her to the ground with gentleness reserved for only this type of occasion.

The elevator crept up to the second floor and Katie, as best she could, maneuvered down the hall. After obeying the number signs on the wall, she turned to the right. Katie slipped through the door and there he was… Eyes closed, skin like a bathroom shower curtain, tubes running here and there, two or three screens on the wall behind his bed. She knew they were blinking bad news.

There was a small guy wearing doctor garb and the obligatory stethoscope around his neck. He turned to face Katie. Was this really happening? This thought went across her mind like strung lights. She thought she was looking at Joe Walsh and half expected him to break out into "Life's been Good," but he didn't.

The doctor's words laid out the nails for the coffin. "Katie, Jack had a massive heart attack. He is holding on by his fingertips. I don't know of anything we can do at this point. I have already gotten a second and third opinion and they concur. I am very sorry."

Katie felt as if a vortex had been created in the room but she was the only one being spun around. "How much time does he have?"

The doctor looked into her eyes and said "It could be fifteen minutes or fifteen hours. It is just a question of when he wants to let go."

Katie had thoughts that came like jackhammers on concrete. Jack was going to die. She remembered when Enos died how Maryellen had time with him that she still cherished each and every day. This was her time with Jack and no one else… She said nothing.

Maryellen, appeared in the room and held Katie's hand and pointed with her free finger at each person in the room and then flicked it towards the door. She did not need to say anything. They all left including the doc. She then whispered to Katie. "Baby, call me when you need me. I will be close." They shared a quick hug, Maryellen shut the door on her way out.

Katie pulled a chair to the bed and held Jack's hand. It felt like it was made of thin cold paper, but as she held it, his forefinger tremored as if to say hello. She did not know what to do or say, but Jack took care of that. "Katie, I can't see but I know it is you. I feel better now."

While all of this was going on, Katie had one thing she had to say and she did not want to waste time just telling Jack she loved him. "Jack, I apologized to Maryellen this morning and I am apologizing to you now. Apologizing to Maryellen was not easy but she is my friend. You are my lover and partner. I jeopardized us. Please forgive me if it the last thing you do." Immediately, she regretted saying "the last thing."

Jack opened his eyes and said, "Move some of this shit out of the way and lay in the bed with me. I knew this was going to happen and I am good with it. I have had time to prepare. Katie, I want to tell you how I feel about you and I do forgive you. You were just being a pompous ass and we all do that upon occasion...You, much less than most." He tried to continue but could not. His breathing was irregular, sometimes like a rapid stutter and others like a slow drawn out wheeze.

Katie had already made the decision not to tell Jack about Kasein. If he asked, that would require another quick decision.

She maneuvered some of the tubes around, lowered the side bars and wiggled into the bed with Jack. His breathing slowed as if he was relaxing and he spoke again, labored but clear.

"Katie, I have done a lot of things in my life, some good, some bad and some I never want to bring to the surface. My lot in life is that I have done a lot of things good, I was a pretty good basketball player in high school. Same with baseball. I did reasonably good as an attorney, but the common thread through all my endeavors was that I was just good. Not great at anything, with one exception... I loved you great. My love for you transformed my entire being. You gave every day a chance of success. I knew that whatever I did, it carried a banner of integrity and honor. The last two years of my life, I walked with my head held high. Simply because I was a great lover of Katie and it really pisses me off that I am going to die." This speech wore him out, he gasped for breath and closed his eyes.

Katie drug this through a mull pasture and said in reply, "Jack, you have carried yourself in splendid fashion each and every day that we have been together. You told me something one time about your father. How a business acquaintance of his told you that your dad had moxie. Well you have moxie. Your gift was your presence."

"One other thing, your entry into the body farm. Have you signed the papers?

He nodded his head like it weighed fifty pounds.

"I am going to take that as a yes. Maryellen, Renfroe, Cherie and I are all going to drive you up. Is it ok if their partners come with? We think it only fitting that we all go. There will be music, food, and alcohol. The three necessities of life for you and me. The only thing missing will be sex. It will be a love caravan, not a dirge caravan. You will be proud."

The last part of this was the recipient of a receding smile from Jack. It was as if someone had tied strings to the connector point of his upper and lower lip and then lifted those connections just ever so slightly. Katie had a terrible thought. He looks like The Joker. That was the best he could do. His pain was deep and it came to visit more often as time wore on.

This type of conversation went on for what seemed like forever. Jack would doze off and shiver every once in a while. Katie scooted up in the bed so that she could bring Jack's head to nestle against her neck with her arm around his upper body. She wanted to cover him up and lay on top of him as if she could protect him from the death that floated above the bed. No one interrupted them. Katie knew that Maryellen had positioned herself outside the door and brought forward a countenance that said, "Don't even try it."

Stuff was going on outside the room. Ruby had ghosted in like a wraith, she just appeared. Renfroe gathered in a feeling of relief so he would be able to share in his upcoming tasks. He spoke to her aside from the group and told her what they were faced with. She just took his hand and started walking down the hall to the elevators. She was a practitioner of peace and practicality in all situations.

—— • • • ——

Amelia was standing in the yard as they rolled Kasein into the back of the hearse. As Renfroe and Ruby approached, she was crying and just testifying to the earth. "She was my best friend, she told me this might happen, but that kind of info, you just put away in a mental storage bin and don't think about it. I don't know you. I am Amelia."

"I am Renfroe and this is my wife, Ruby. Do you know about Jack and Katie?"

"Yes, I do. I also know who you are. Kasein and I were very close. She told me the whole thing. I think I was the only person she told all of this information to. During the entire afternoon when she told me, I kept thinking how she was like a little girl in her first and only dance recital. This is just terrible."

Ruby spoke up. "Where is Kalia? We came over at the request of Katie. Jack is in the hospital in very bad condition. He is not expected to live out the day."

"She is inside with my daughter. They are very close in age and friendship. I don't know if she has grasped the fact that her mother passed or not."

Renfroe stepped in with his official voice. "Do you know if Kasein had made any arrangements with a funeral home? Katie wants us to bring Kalia back with us if possible. I think it would be a good idea for you and Ruby to go and talk with her. If she wants to, can she stay with you for a couple of days or so?"

Amelia answered, "Yes, Kasein made all the arrangements, cremation was her choice. She had paid for it and taken care of everything. Of course, Kalia can stay as long as she wants. I don't know if you were aware that Jack came over last week and met with Kasein. Kasein told Jack about her medical prognosis and she was surprised to find out that he had the same deal. It is hereditary. I know that she does not have any relatives and that she and Jack talked about Kalia. I think they made some type of commitment that Jack and Katie were to take care of Kalia in case of this happening."

Renfroe slightly nodded in agreement, "Yes, they agreed that Jack and Katie would step up and take Kalia. Jack called me earlier this week and told me to get documents ready for this. The docs are ready but unsigned. Why don't we see how Kalia is doing before we get into the wherefores of the situation?"

Amelia took Ruby's hand and they walked into the house, while

Renfroe got on his phone and called Maryellen. He brought her up to date on the previous conversation and asked about Jack.

Renfroe was looking at the sky which was lazuline in tone and thought what a beautiful day for these leavings to happen almost at the same time. He knew he was going to miss Jack; the words Kayak Talk was present in his mind like a theater marquee. He would not have that privilege ever again.

He was standing by his car and looked like a man counting rosary beads when Ruby, Amelia, Kalia and Amelia's daughter walked out the front door. Kalia was holding Ruby's hand like she belonged there. Many times, a six-year-old child escapes being hammered by a death knell. The price of that ability would be paid for many times over in later life.

Ruby walked right by Renfroe and entered the car, leaving the following message hanging in the air like clothes on a line. "Kalia wants to go to be with Katie, her mother told her that is what she was to do if anything happened to her."

Renfroe like a private car driver, got in the car and off they went. Amelia and her daughter were holding hands and waved good bye.

Renfroe knew he might be on shaky ground from a legal standpoint by taking Kalia but he would cross that hard road when he got to it and hope some legal goat was not around to make things difficult.

———— ♦ ♦ ♦ ————

The day toddled on in little baby steps and Jack had not said anything for a long while. Katie was startled as Jack raised his head and spoke in a firm voice. "Baby, do you remember that time we were making love and I stopped in midstroke? You said what is wrong? Did I do something? I answered, I am just tired and rolled away. That is happening again. Baby, I am really tired. I love you and goodbye."

JACK LEAVES
THE BUILDING

KATIE OPENED THE DOOR in the middle of the afternoon and said. "Jack just left us." The rest of the crew had seen her come out the door and hustled to become a closed circle.

Katie spoke in strong voice that was brought up from way down, "Jack looked at me and said. I love you and goodbye, and he let his fingertips release the ledge."

Her body folded as if she were made of small tiles and they tilted one into another, until she fell. Toliver stepped quickly forward and caught her in his arms. She recovered slowly, then said, "Would you all like to go in and say good bye? I am sure he would like that."

Maryellen leaned in and whispered to Katie, "Renfroe and Ruby will be here in a few minutes. They have Kalia, she wanted to be with you."

Katie spoke in elegiac tones. "I want to be with her. You know that I am going to need your help going forward'"

Maryellen gave a nod that layered many depths of 'yes'.

Cherie went first, she did not stay long, but when she came out, she was smiling. The conversation had gone like this. "Jack, I will miss you like a foxhole buddy. You know things about me that need to die along with you. It is a rare relationship that you and I shared. It just doesn't happen often between the tittied and the non-tittied. I will keep a special stash in my life only for you, way past the time when I become a fat little old lady. Trip and I will always be a safe haven for Katie. Do not worry about her. Have a smooth ride." She walked out with a smile on her face and said "I fluffed him up for the rest of you girly girls." Then she retreated under the arm of Trip. "That was too soon wasn't it?" Trip gave a slight nod, but not big enough to hurt her feelings.

Renfroe was standing at the edge of the circle with Ruby. Ruby was the crutch that Renfroe needed from time to time and this was one of those times.

Renfroe knew something no one else in the group was privy to. Jack had come to see him on Wednesday night and they had sat out on the deck, drank a beer and talked. His visit had been unannounced until Jack had called him from his truck parked in front of Renfroe's house. "Renfroe, can I come in for a few minutes?"

In one fraction, Jack was walking through his front door. A phrase ran through his mind. Jack looked like he was made of mismatched pieces that did not fit right. His demeanor was not the usual straight up Jack. Renfroe knew things were unarranged and weird.

Jack sat in his chair, as if he were taking a picture of the dark. Renfroe said, "What's up?" and left that hanging in the air like a smoke ring.

Jack just sat there, until an almost undiscernible tremelo moved through his entire body and he spoke. "Renfroe, this is tandem kayak talk. I will pre-apologize for this, but I have weighed all the people I know and you topped the scales to be appointed for a special assignment. I am dying, and I don't mean in a long time. I mean you might have to watch me die in a few minutes."

Renfroe felt a sound roll through his body like a moving vibration. It said, "God no, please God no." Sadness, disbelief, and shock came as one mighty thrust that almost took him down. He could not say anything.

Jack continued, "This afternoon, the doc delivered the news like a substitute mailman. He just wanted to get through it." Jack reached in his pocket and took out a sheaf of papers and gave them to Renfroe. "There are directions for a going away party. It has fallen your lot to read my goodbye at my shindig. It is not long, but I want it read by you. Good night, my friend."

He disappeared around the corner of the house as if he had already started to wear the clothes of the dead. It was like he had not even been there. Renfroe sat there as if he were made of old bricks and any movement would have caused him to crumble.

Ruby came out and took his hand and led him inside for the night. She said nothing. She knew nothing. She could tell there was nothing to say.

Renfroe's entry into the hospital room was reminiscent of a very old man, he did not want to look at Jack. He did not want to witness the subtraction of vibrancy that had been Jack. Renfroe wanted to go home and have a big drink of scotch, very good scotch. He leaned over the bed and with his hand he reached over to Jack's head. He looked like he did not know what he was doing, but he touched Jack with a tenderness that might only be in evidence towards a new born child. Renfroe said nothing. It had all been said and the bond was not broken. As he walked out the door, something his dad had said to him rang like a church bell in his mind. "A man who loses a true friend has lost a treasure."

Maryellen and Katie were standing together with their heads touching to form a small tent. Their hands were helt together and the picture only said one word: nestling. Kalia stood between them, her head looking up alternating back and forth. Katie gave Maryellen a small push in the back. Maryellen looked over her shoulder and looked at Toliver as if to say, I will not be long, so don't leave.

She walked into the room and wore the darkness like it had been made just for her. "Jack, you know that I did not like you when I first met you, but it was only because I looked at you like a snake in the grass. In my mind, you could do no good for my friend Katie. I remember one night when we all were making a team effort on the whiskey world, you said to me 'Maryellen, you always look at me like my mother would when she caught me in a lie.' Jack, you had all the potential for a pandemic of pain. I whiffed on that diagnosis and was glad to be held accountable. I knew your past to be more checkered than a Purina feed sack. Watching Katie with you was like watching a potter throw an artisanal vase using the remains from an old mud hole. I thank you for being Katie's lover. I also thank you for not being mine. You and I took a horribly designed theatric script and rewrote the lines into a happy ending. Tell Enos that I miss him terribly. I will always carry the torch for him, but Toliver is a man that can deliver the goods."

She reached down and held his cool hand as if it would break. "A demain, Jack." She walked out the door into the arms of the whitest man in town.

The only sound to be heard was the squeak of a nurse's shoes as she scurried up the hallway. Katie looked at her congregation with beatification in mind. She had swum away from not being able to accept Jack's leaving her, being mad at him for the loneliness she would acquire and having no one to use her toes as piano keys. Peace engulfed her. She stood on the podium with a gold medal that would last her forever. "Why don't you all go to my house and I will see you later. There are a few things I want to tell Jack and I am sure he has had time to think about what to say to me." She leaned down and said, "Kalia, stay with Maryellen and Toliver, I will be there in just a little bit."

Katie opened the door and went away. Mumbling was the predominant noise until Toliver assumed the reins and asked, "Maryellen, do you want to stay and drive her home? I'll stay with you. We can all go home in my car."

Maryellen without answering his question directly, spoke to Ruby. "Would you and Renfroe take Kalia with you. I am going to stay with Katie. Tolliver will drive us home."

Ruby did not say a word, just reached down and took Kalia by the hand.

Renfroe, Ruby and Kalia walked down the hall away from the watchful eye of Maryellen as she thought to herself. Now that couple does not sing a love dirge.

Cherie and Trip walked away without a word.

Katie's peace shattered like her grandmother's falling coffee cup as she opened the door to Jack's room. He was still there and he had not retracted his final letter of resignation. He seemed to have shrunk just in the short time she had been out of the room. She knew this was her time to say good bye. She also knew she had to tell Jack about Kasein. Jack we are now officially grandparents. Kasein died this morning.

Kalia is now our child. I will keep you informed. Maybe you and Kasein will be together, who knows?"

Katie and Jack had always said the time they spent sitting, talking and listening to good music was the best, sex was great but their shared discourse was the anchor of their being. Their conversations were as wide ranging as a global map.

They could have been riding around in the car on Saturday afternoon and making fun of people. Katie remembered the last time she and Jack had done that. They saw this guy walking down the sidewalk, the man's upper body was twisted to the left and his leading shoulder was about six inches above the other one, his feet were way too small for the rest of his body. The man's chin was tucked into his leading shoulder and his walk could only be characterized as darting. Katie had shouted, "There goes Louis from Suits."

Most of their sit downs were on the back porch. She sat at her old round table and he sat in a rocking chair...The music was always good. She could think of no other word to describe those times other than fun. They enjoyed each other like a child with a new toy every day. There were no down days, neither would allow the other to crawl on the ground. All of this was etched in her mind like words on a tombstone. These thoughts would be her companions forever.

She knew that Maryellen had stayed with Enos for several hours even after he died, but Katie knew that Jack would have none of that. It was time to go. Things had to be done. Jack was gone.

Katie walked out the door with no purpose at all... She was floundering. Death is cunning in that it still won't let you believe it happened and she knew there would be many mornings that in that split second of wakefulness she would reach for him and the bed would be cold. She might walk into the kitchen and reach out her hand to take the cup of coffee Jack always had at the ready for her. She would get in the shower and wonder why he hadn't pulled back the curtain and come into the warmth with her. Going to work, she would catch a glance of him in his truck going in the opposite direction. Getting a phone call at work and the voice on the other end mimicked the sound of Jack, and so on and so on. All of these things would come to her like a light stroke on a triangle of loneliness, sorrow and sometimes joy. She knew his presence would linger like a rung bell, but time might cause him to fade like the end of a song.

She walked to the waiting car, got in and was held by Maryellen like a tiny doll.

What time was it? She just knew that it was dark and suddenly she was hungry. Jack would be proud. He was always worried about her not eating enough or properly. By that he meant eating often, a lot and good stuff. It was 8:55 P.M. Good, it was late enough that nobody would stay long and she could go to bed. She was wrong, the word had spread and the house was wide awake.

Katie walked into the house, took Kalia in tow and walked straight to her bedroom. She had already bought clothes for Kalia during the previous week. She shuffled through boxes until she found some pajamas. "Kalia, come her baby. Let's put these p.j.s on you, do you want to sleep in here with me tonight. I wish you would, I am going to be lonely." Kalia said nothing, just started putting on the pajamas. When they were on, she crawled into the waiting bed.

Katie thought she knew everybody, but she needn't worry. Maryellen was with her like the Secret Service. Whoever wanted to speak with her got two to three minutes then hustled away for the next in line. Food appeared from who knows where, and alcohol flowed like silent rain. Katie and Maryellen alternated checking on Kalia, she was always sound asleep.

Stories were told and the phrase, "Remember that time that we," was predominant the entire night. Katie heard stories told as the gospel truth that Jack had told her had never happened. Stories were told for the umpteenth time and she thought she would break out screaming if someone told the one about his jumping off a bridge one more time.

Maryellen played the part of a helicopter friend right up to the time when she whispered to Katie, "Let's go to bed," and she steered Katie towards the bedroom and the people parted as if the Queen of England was coming through. People stopped in midstory, couples reached for the hand of their partner, glasses were tipped up to take that last swallow and it was like watching a silent movie of people leaving a room.

Toliver told Maryellen, "Good night, call me if you need me, and I will be here in the morning to cook breakfast."

Maryellen walked through the house, turning off all the lights and putting a few things in the sink. She approached the bedroom door with trepidation as she had no idea what to expect. What she got was total silence and two bodies on the bed. If Katie had been vertical, she would have looked like a sprinter in mid stride. The normal reaction took place and Maryellen started to tiptoe across the room.

The silence broke slowly as Katie spoke in a toneless voice. "If no one had told me that Jack was gone, I still would know it. There is no music. With Jack, there was always music. Would you que up the Bluetooth and play the Revivalist radio? He would like that.

Kate and Maryellen lay on each side of Kalia in the bed and both would sing along as they knew most of the words. Both of them were having the same reminiscence and both had the same crooked smile on their face. They were remembering Enos and Jack who both liked singing along with music, but neither knew all the words. That deficit caused no reduction in enthusiasm or volume for either one of them. Maryellen could feel Katie's desire to talk.

"Maryellen, in one day, I have become a widow and a full-time grandmother. I am going to miss Jack and you are the only one who knows the depth of surrounding sorrow in my life. The curious thing is I keep remembering vignettes in our life together and most of them are funny. I remember one time when Jack and I were having one of our fake arguments. He told me that he was cutting me off on Monday, Tuesday, Wednesday afternoon, Thursday, unless it was a holiday and Friday until five o'clock in the afternoon. Saturday and Sunday were open sex days. There will never be another Jack Riordan."

She shut her eyes, lightly caressed Kalia's tiny brow.

"Maryellen, you know you are going to be co-grandmother."

"Katie, I would not have it any other way. I jumped off the dock and into that boat early today."

Anyone who might have been out for a walk that night and passed Katie and Jack's house would have seen a house as dark as ink and would have heard the sounds of "Souls too Loud" decorating the darkness like last year's Christmas ornaments.

THE DAYS AFTER

TOLIVER WALKED INTO THE room, he briefly thought about saying, "Good morning, widows and orphans," but quickly retracted that idea. One of them might have thought it funny, but the other one would not and the third would not understand it. He settled on, "It is a bright sunshiny day, and I have the lubricant to start the morning…Coffee, Ladies. Fixed exactly like you desire. I have bagels in the toaster, cream cheese, honey, vegan butter and lingonberry jam for your selection. I can add eggs benedict if you would like or you can stay with the bagels. Your choice."

Maryellen sat on the edge of the bed as if she was running a check list on her body parts just to see if they were all there and in good working order. Enos ran across her mind like Flash Gordon and he did not leave the yearn that usually accompanied his mental videos… Progress? Yes, progress. She stood up and walked over to and gave Toliver a tiny kiss but one that had value. He smiled, turned on his heel, did something that men usually don't do, he floated out of the room. The Swabbie and Librarian relationship had taken on strength and risen like a good cake.

Katie woke several times during the night, but they were slim traces of time and she went back to sleep. She was fully awake now but stayed horizontal. The sadness had hit her like dynamite. The strength of it was ungodly. She tried to get up and walk, but fell to her knees on the floor and cried as if her soul was being torn into little pieces. Now she understood the sorrow that had consumed Maryellen.

Katie was still on her knees with her head hung between her

shoulders. Her eyes opened like they didn't want to but they recognized the four feet in front of her. Maryellen reached with both hands and Katie grasped them like lifelines and stood up. Kalia was wrapped around one leg...Silence was all there was to hear. They stood like three mannequins until Maryellen broke the spell. She walked over to the closet and returned with two dressing gowns. Katie opened a new box and produced a little girl's bathrobe, that fit like a charm.

When they walked into the kitchen area, all three were holding hands. They looked like two teenage girls and a little sister walking in the waves at the beach... Chatting was the only word to describe their discourse.

Toliver had assumed the stance of a chef working a buffet line for brunch. He asked, "Eggs fried, scrambled or omelets."

"Neither," was their answer. "Bagels will suffice this morning."

A small voice asked, "Do you have any Captain Crunch?"

Tolliver, reached under the counter and produced an unopened box of the Captain's finest Crunch. He got a "Thank you sir" in return.

Katie said, "I don't know who, but I am sure we will be subject to invasion by nattily dressed wives, sisters and mothers today. It's the thing to do, you know. I have to grow into becoming a widowbird. Do I have to wear black all the time or just at funereal events? I shall not wear black all the time. Speaking of services, what are we going to do?"

The doorbell rang, Maryellen went to answer and the usual group had one hundred percent attendance. Renfroe, Ruby, Cherie, and Trip at the door. They had Katie's favorite doughnuts. That made her cry as it was usually Jack who brought them to her. They even had one Bismarck with white filling and chocolate on top, that was her favorite. Her cry was a small cry.

The four of them looked like they had an agenda. It was a strange group, the four of them stood like undertakers stand, hands together in front, faces forward.

All but Ruby, she took Kalia by the hand and said "Let's get you dressed and then we will take a walk down to the park." In less than three minutes, she and Kalia were out the door.

Renfroe broke the silence. "Katie, we know that all decisions are yours, but we all loved Jack and we would like to be part of the process.

I, for one, was given an assignment pre-death by Jack. Last Wednesday night Jack came over to my house. He told me he was going to die soon and he wanted me to read the letter he gave me. He said he wanted it read at a gathering, which he called Sign off Soiree. Katie, I know this is early on and quite presumptuous of me. I am only the humble messenger."

Jack said to me. "We have to do it quick and it wouldn't matter to him if no one comes but us. The velocity of all this is dictated by his appointment with the body farm. We do not have the luxury, if you could call it that, of waiting until the weekend." An uneasy pall cast itself on the group, but just for a second. Renfroe continued.

"Jack now resides in a very uncomfortable wood box in the death parlor. The schedule of events, as suggested by the funeral folks, is to have the soiree tomorrow night and delivery to the body farm on Wednesday. I apologize again for the bluntness of this presentation and its timing, but Jack was adamant in his directives to me."

Twelve eyes focused on the lady Katie. There is much difficulty in describing a person who seems to be captured in the throes of laughing, sadness and decision making, all at once. Convoluted might be a start to describe Katie. She stood tall and said, 'I think we should have the soiree right here. All of you can ask anyone you like or don't like. Just make sure they would be an addition to the affair. Jack had a few relatives, a brother in California, three cousins scattered from Texas to Colorado to right here. I'll try to contact them.

"Renfroe, do you have any of the finer details? You just gave us the broad outline. I'm asking about food, drink, music, etcetera, or did Jack leave those items to our discretion?" Renfroe confirmed that Jack only gave a broad outline.

Katie spoke as if she had spent a decade planning her speech for this event. Many times in the future, the attendees said that she spoke like his death and post events were things she had prepared for like a PTA president. "Let's start with the thing that will be the hardest to organize, food. Toliver would you cook meat? Ribs were Jack's favorite. One of the mysteries of southern life is how a potluck dinner always feeds everyone in great fashion. I say, we start a new tradition, a potluck dinner to celebrate the walking away of one of God's blessings, my man Jack.

"As for the libations. Renfroe, you're the most accomplished drinker I know. I will give you my credit card and you handle it. My only caveat is that you buy from a liquor store that will deliver in case we start to run short in mid-soiree.

"The music is mine. I definitely will need a little help with the electronics and sound.

"Cherie and Trip, you might be getting the hardest assignment. I do not want any argument against this request. I want you both to figure out how to bring Jack in the Box to the soiree. He would demand to be here. Toliver and Maryellen, would you organize the house, tables, chairs, in other words set up the backyard. Make sure there is room to dance. Any questions?"

Renfroe's best effort was a series of "Uh, uh, uh. There is one thing I have not mentioned. Jack also gave me a recording of him singing a song. Copies of the words are printed out. He wanted the song to be played and have everyone sing along with him. I am not to reveal the song but he has given me karaoke directions."

This declaration caused total participation in smiles as it was an unspoken joke among his friends that, "Jack could not sing worth a shit." The only people who sing worse than him was his high school quarterback and his ex-wife. Jack was under the impression that he was an undiscovered rock and roll star. The conventional wisdom was that the only way for him to get close to the stage with a rock and roll band was for him to buy a front row ticket. The smiles were contained by much effort, but not for long as laughter escaped like air out of an old balloon.

Katie recovered and said, "Well, we have let him dictate the course so far, so let's get that done. Renfroe and Ruby are in charge of that directive. One other thing. All of you are invited to participate in the deliverance of Jack to the body farm. It's a long ride and I have to find a vehicle that will hold the box. It may require a trailer. I'm open to suggestions."

Trip ruptured the silence. "I would like the honor of being in charge of the transportation to the body farm. I have some ideas on that front. I also have connections in the transportation business."

Cherie smiled and said, "He doesn't say a lot, but when he does it counts."

Katie said, "Thank you, Trip. That part is in your hands."

Katie noticed Ruby coming out of the bedroom by herself. "Ruby, could you stick around here and talk with Maryellen and me for a while. I almost forgot."

The three of them got another cup of coffee and sat on the sofa.

Katie began in a normal voice but it wilted in mid-sentence. "Ruby, I have no idea what to do about Kalia. There has never been a child to even spend the night in my house. Now I have a six-year-old grandchild whose mother just died along with my husband." The emotional weight ripped her body until she looked boneless. Katie fell over on the sofa and cried deep wheels of anguish that would not stop rolling. Maryellen held her like a mother holds her child. The three did not talk or move. Then it was over as if a door slammed shut.

"How is Kalia? I haven't really had time to have a private conversation with her."

The question was plainly directed to Ruby, who answered, "She is doing okay, but she is a six-year-old little girl and she won't be able to get her arms around her mother's death for a while. I think she will have some lonesome times. Remember she and her mother have been a couple for her entire life. The lonesomeness will take a bite out of her life many times going forward. What you have to not do is to try to be her mother. You can't wear those shoes. The more people you can involve in her life would be a good goal at this time, especially other children. Watch her for signs of withdrawal from life, try to keep her in the game."

Katie wanted more.

"What do I do about her school? I know you taught school in the lower grades."

Ruby responded, "It would be harder if she were older. A first grader has not yet established those best buddy bonds. It might be a little rough at first, but that should not be a problem going forward.

I would get her back in school as soon as possible. Do you have any friends who could give you some guidance on where to enroll her?"

Maryellen spoke up, "Let me get that part of the plan. I have two librarians who have children in grammar schools. They should be able to give us some good advice in that selection process."

Katie seemed to revive on this discussion. She knew that she could chew real hard on a problem once it was defined. "Ruby, thank you and I know you need to get going. One more question, I have someone going to her house tomorrow and bring everything in her room over here, I am going to try and replicate her room as close as I can. What do you think?"

Ruby had a short answer. "As Jack would say, super deluxe." And as was her way, she disappeared out the front door with Renfroe attached.

With all departures done. We go back to the widows.

— ◆ ◆ ◆ —

Katie picked up the pace and said, "We need to get dressed, as you well know one of the sacrosanct southern death rituals should begin shortly and we'll need to look the part."

Sure nuf. Just as the three of them were walking out of the bedroom, the doorbell rang. All of them were looking spiffy. Katie had on black long pants with bell bottoms that started at the knee, a white shirt with small collar and buttoned sleeves and of course, a magnificent pearl necklace. Maryellen had on tight blackish green pants with a faint green tee shirt. Kalia rocked a pair of pink polka dotted shorts, topped with a white long-sleeved tee shirt. All were barefooted. Katie and Maryellen were as stunning as double doyennes in a Spanish palace. Kalia had a small smile, she had never considered herself fancy until then.

The parade started and two people at a time came through the door for the next hour or so. All were heavily laden...Fried chicken, deviled eggs, finger sandwiches, pies galore and if there was a souffle invented that wasn't there, it had to have been a mistake. The kitchen counters soon looked like an all you can eat buffet line. Sweet tea, lemonade to mix with the tea, many bottles of wine all of which suffered severe damage almost immediately. All of this was scattered all over the kitchen, but was somehow organized.

Katie moved through and around the room like she was running for county commissioner. Maryellen resumed her role as gatekeeper and everyone got two or three minutes and that was it. Mourners were shuffled away without even knowing they had been dismissed. This was all okay with everyone. They all had participated in this dance before and were well versed in the proper protocol. Katie wore a tight smile which she removed and replaced as necessary. Kalia stayed close.

The ladies shared the latest gossip and swapped partners like square dancers. The big story of the day was started by the wife of one of the county deputy sheriffs. Her tale involved the high sheriff and his latest girlfriend.

The story was originated by said girlfriend who had confessed to one of her friends, who of course was compelled to pass along to one of her friends. It went like this. The sheriff had a nickname that his female companion gave him. She called him 'Jai Alai' because he suffered from the bent dick syndrome and she said his pecker was curved like a cesta. She also referred to their boudoir as "The Fronton." This story got passed along as quickly as a baby with a dirty diaper. The pecker got bigger and more bent with each telling. Truth be told, the deputy sheriff was running for sheriff in the next election.

The afternoon started to wear itself out and the early moon came out of the closet.

Katie disappeared like a blocked shadow. The ladies left in pairs as if their names had been called over a loudspeaker. They gathered in small groups in the front yard and talked of how well Katie looked, how cute the little girl was, what time was the book club Thursday night and who was going to the soiree. The main topic of conversation was the rumor that a lot of the girls were going to wear flannel pajama bottoms and white tee shirts with no bra. The underwriter of that tidbit was none other than Renfroe.

Maryellen and two remainderwomen gathered the dishes, cleaned the counters, threw away the wine bottles, getting it done in military fashion. Again, Maryellen went through the house and turned out all the lights. She then hesitated for an instant and thought of Enos, but it passed.

She started to call Toliver, but didn't, but then did. He was at home and answered on the second ring.

"I was hoping you would call," he said. "How are you doing?"

Maryellen replied like someone who had just gotten the information she needed. "Just checking in. I am fine, will see you in the morning."

———— ◆ ◆ ◆ ————

Maryellen walked into the bedroom as silent as a house cat. The opening chords of "Still Got the Blues" rang true in the dark. Appropriate for the occasion, and there was nothing like it in the world of music. She could see the single profile of Katie in the bed. Kalia must be in the other bedroom. There was a combination of off and on mewling coming from a voice talking as if in conversation with the night. This is what she heard: "Jack, no one really knew, I tried many times to explain it to Maryellen and came close, but no one knew. We had a love that burned like a charcoal ember, while everyone else wore their love like an old jacket against the cold."

Maryellen slid into the bed and put her arms around Katie like you would hold a ten-year-old child in the throes of a nightmare. She could feel shudders course through Katie like spastic waves. She could only say, "Jack knows. He will always be there and he knows."

Maryellen had not been allowed into the garden of deep sleep, so she was not surprised when she heard Katie whispering to her, "Do you think he's ok. You know he did not believe The Hand of the universe meddled in everything. He thought you just died and that was it, nothing else."

Words crawled out of Katie's mouth. "I cannot walk my belief down that path. People look at us walk down the street and we are placed in that crate of the aged. We are diminished, our abilities are barely above decrepit, we are functionally frail. How could that be? You and I were drenched in the deepest love affairs of our lives at sixty something. It just doesn't add up. There has to be something else. Maybe we were being shown something like the previews at a movie. I know I will see

Jack again and this time it will not be interrupted by dying. I am going with that for as long as I breathe. Now I have to sleep. Tomorrow is a big day and the next day we are going to deliver Jack's shell to the body farm. Good night. I'll be okay in the morning."

Maryellen murmured, "Tell him to find Enos and tell him I am doing well. I have a friend who is a good man, but Enos still bats cleanup in my lineup. I will see him soon."

Morning came right on time and brought Toliver with it. He had been in the house a good while, so when he came into the bedroom, he had excellent roasted coffee. He carried it on a silver tray, the whitest of creams, cubes of sugar and a matched pair of cups and saucers. Maryellen learned later that Toliver had brought those over from his house. They had been his grandmother's...Even before she discovered that fact, she said to herself, "That boy keeps scoring points."

The girls walked into the room, Katie and Maryellen were each wearing a set of Katie's silk pajamas. Kalia followed looking like a miniature replication of the others. Toliver thought to himself, why is it that sometimes soft, smooth loose-fitting clothes drop hints of erotica that tight jeans or little bathing suits can't even talk about. He then reminded himself he was cooking for two widows and cooking was his key to the kingdom this morning.

The breakfast presented itself in tasteful colors and dense aromas. Eggs over easy with perfect circular whites and yellows that needed no description, bowls of unusual fruits, pieces of toast cut in thin sheets, blueberry pancakes with strawberries sleeping on top, warmed honey and bacon thick but cooked to crispiness and no further. If Toliver's mother had been there, she would have said only one word. "Scrumptious," and it was. Talking left the room. Again.

The morning did a slow waltz to the noon time hour. People were in and out of the house with no schedule. They were like stagehands between acts. They all seemed purposeful in their goings and comings. Katie was absent from all the activity and stayed in the bedroom with Kalia. Maryellen would check on her from time to time. Katie asked, "What is going on out there? Do I need to do anything?"

Maryellen just waved her hand like a dismissing royal and answered the question, "No, just enjoy your widowhood. Shit is getting done."

Katie stretched out on the bed and felt eyes on her, she turned her head and was confronted by a little girl's face adorned with tears. Kalia was trying to talk but words were trapped inside like prisoners. Katie only needed to say a few words. "Come here baby. You know that you and are partners like no one else. It is you and me from now on. Do you have anything you want to ask me?"

"Is my momma dead?"

Katie thought, young lady you are your mother's child. "Yes, your mother has gone to be with my husband Jack. I am sure they are looking at both of us right this minute. Your grandfather is saying something like 'suck it up girls, Kasein and I are fine and we will be keeping an eye on you from now on.' Your mother is telling you how much she loves you and that you are going to be loved like no other little girl in the world." Katie continued in another vein, "There is something else I need to ask you. I want you to live with me, I should have asked you sooner, but is that okay with you."

"Yes ma'am, I would like that."

"One other thing, I am having everything in your bedroom delivered here, we are going to arrange your room just like it was at home. You and I have to take care of each other and I want you to come to me anytime you need to, I don't care what is going on or what time of the day or night, you come get Katie."

That got a star sparkle in Kalia's eye and a smile on her face.

The afternoon had advanced the pace to a samba. Toliver worked diligently over his ribs. He had done all of the calculations as to how many and how long. He was approaching the time for the coals to be lit. The ribs were hand rubbed and ready for the grill.

Renfroe had called on his spiderweb of friends and the sound system was in place. A dance floor appeared out of nowhere. Chairs were brought by friends all through the afternoon. Tables were absconded from churches and schools.

Ruby had assumed the position of director. She gave quick orders on placement of everything from food to table covers. At a later time, Ruby said she had to take over direction to keep Renfroe from making a big mess of the whole thing. It was going to be stupendous. Jack would be happy.

Things slowed in the leftovers of daylight. Katie had said one of the mysteries of life was how a covered dish to-do always worked out. This one was no exception. It was like a directive had been issued to everyone as to what to bring. It was perfect. Diversification and balance were the orders of the day. Five dishes of roasted asparagus did not happen.

During that time when the sun has disappeared, but there was still light, everyone stopped moving as if someone had pulled their plug from the wall.

A very long limousine pulled into the driveway with a trailer in tow. The limousine was funeral black, but the trailer was another thing altogether. It was a box trailer about eight feet long. A refugee from another time must have been the artist who painted the trailer. It was one hundred percent psychedelic, freshly done with the letters B.O.B. on both sides. The translation flew through the crowd instantly, "Body on Board". No one moved, the music stopped playing. Trip stepped from the driver's side of the limo; Cherie came around to him. Katie came out the back door of the house, took one look at the trailer, another look at the frozen bodies and said, "Someone needs to get his ass out of that trailer."

Trip opened the back door of the trailer and there was at least ten people on both sides of the sex equinox gathered to help. There were rope handles on the box, which were quickly grabbed by self-appointed pall bearers who placed it on two sawhorses that Renfroe had borrowed from a construction site. The box was plain wood and shaped like it came out of an old western movie.

It was like no one knew what to do, but someone turned on the music and activity resumed. The honored guest was present and the party which had no times announced went from purposeful activities to party time as the early nighttime took over the helm.

Someone had brought heavy markers and soon the box was covered with graffiti. Some of it fit to read and some not.

Music gathered players like an eclectic seine. The gamut was deep and wide. The crux of the music carried a common thread. It had to be danceable. Dancing was sporadic and the whiskey brought out the non- dancers by the second hour. The in crowd watched and murmured to each other, "Nothing more painful than watching people dance who can't dance."

Ribs were down to the last rack, not much remained except for some brussel sprouts. Katie said "Who the hell would bring brussel sprouts to a fine occasion like this?"

Renfroe had obtained a microphone at the last minute. He had been judging the crowd for just the right moment for him to introduce Jack's good bye.

Katie had talked with him about the timing and made it plain. She did not want him exposing Jack to a bunch of drunks. She had a quick vision of herself following in the footsteps of Maryellen and being protective of her man's legacy. People would talk about this for years and years, but she did not want it to be seen as a foolish prank.

Renfroe stood next to the box and tapped on the mic for everyone's attention. "Jack and Katie are happy to see everyone here tonight. This "Sign off Soiree" was at the request of Jack. A few nights ago, Jack came by my house and told me of his condition. He planned all of this recently. Part of his coming to see me was that he gave me a missive to read to everyone. He said to tell you that he had never been a standup comedian and could not start tonight as he will be flat on his back. He noticed movement out of the corner of his eye, Katie appeared like a sylph at his side.

Katie had on a classic black sheath and Jack's favorite shoes ballerina pumps. At first, she stood still as stone with her head down as if she was looking at the ground for guidance. She raised her head, then gave her hair a quick flip as if she was shaking raindrops off her face. She took the mic from Renfroe's hand and started to speak.

Her voice was as clear as night air. "I could not let this end without saying a few words about my best friend and lover, Jack Riordan. Jack will continue to be my shelter from the storm. I can feel him like a warm blanket each minute of the day. I will miss him like none other and consider myself to be well blessed to have been linked with Jack for the best time of my life. If you are lucky enough to have this in your life, rub every minute until it is like a polished stone. Thank you Jack, for your opening my life to bright lights and easy air. Au Demain."

She handed the mic back to Renfroe and appeared back at the side of Maryellen and Kalia.

Like a seasoned pro, Renfroe calmly said, "If all of you would refresh your drinks, pull up a chair or sit on the grass. I will read from the Book of Jack."

"I am stealing a line from Dishwalla. 'Tell me all of your thoughts on God' because there is a good chance, I might bump into him in the next few days. Or not. Don't worry because this is not going to drag on and on. I don't know what day of the week this will occur, but I know you might have work tomorrow.

"I wandered through the greater part of my life like a color-blind guy getting dressed. My dad would say I was a big galoot. I just did what was there without any thought of success or failure. Just something or anything that was laying out there for me to pick up and put in my pocket. That all came to a screeching halt when I found the Easter egg with a prize inside. Life became a high definition screen with surround sound. You might wonder how this alchemy happened, it was at the hand of my best friend and lover. She took a lump of clay and polished that boy into a presentable human being. She also brought along a supporting troupe of angels.

"These angels were my friends; they gave me an interpretation of the rule book for friends. Until then I always felt there was a permanent stain on my soul and that my actions were always predicated on my well-being. I learned that genuine joy is best achieved when shared with someone else.

"Thereby, giving me a shot at having those golden years that you often hear referred to for mature adults. I often thought that phrase really meant that as an oldster you were constantly getting pissed on by someone, in a figurative sense, of course. The government, your health or several other facets of the gray life.

"Along came Katie. Her approach to life is to take a bite out of each apple. One time after a less than spectacular sexual event, she said to me, 'Jack, you have to realize this about mature sex. You don't always know what you are going to get, but you should be happy with what you got. I think that without knowing it, she applied that to her whole life and that is where the alchemy kicked in on me.

"Then along came Kasein and Kalia. They are another reason that I hate it that I am writing this letter to everyone. Katie and I missed a lot in our life by not finding each other until late, but we also missed the parent thing. I would like to have gotten into that batter's box and taken a swing at it.

"I am walking the plank to maudlinism. I am going to wrap this up by saying thank you to Katie and her band of angels. My friend Renfroe has set up something for me that all of you will have to suffer through. I have been aware for a long time that there was very nasty and unfair talk about my singing, but I can truly sing. There is a song that has been my favorite song for as long as I can remember. 'Queen of Hearts' by Greg Allman on the album Laid Back. Renfroe has set up this for karaoke, so I am asking all of you to sing along. Sing loud, because Maryellen once told me that my singing was like I discovered my voice in a lost and found bin."

As the inviting guitar opened the door to the song, it was a caressing of the evening time. Jack's voice lived up to Katie's description. Katie stood with her head bowed at first but with a quick shake of her head she became erect. This was repeated many times. People would swear that a circle of light surrounded her. Maryellen held her arm as the song progressed to its end.

Jack would have been proud. Looking through the crowd, couples held hands and would give each other quick glances of love, that maybe had not occurred for a long time. There were not many love dirges as described by Enos. The song ended and people drifted out. They did not know where they were going, but knew they had to leave. It was a splendid event and the music played on.

———— ♦ ♦ ♦ ————

Katie and Maryellen walked up to the box and just stood there wordless. Katie lifted the lid and said, "He looks good." At that moment, they both felt like they were the only people in the entire world. Everyone else had faded into the darkness.

Maryellen with a lilt in her voice said, "I think he has a smile on his face."

Katie and Maryellen both at the same time felt a tiny hand creep into theirs.

As if on cue, Lowdown started to play, Katie turned to Maryellen and Kalia. It was Katie's turn this time, "Will the two of you dance with me?"

The immediate answers came as an utterance of love. "Of course," and they did.

A skinny rain accompanied the morning as it crept through the tired darkness. Katie and Maryellen lay on their backs and seemed to breathe in unison. That was not the only thing in unison, both were being entertained by mental videos of their long-gone boyfriends. That was where the commonality took another fork in the road. Maryellen, being the semi-slut that she was, was riding the sex train with the man formerly known as Enos. She was having a grand time as fornication fantasies teased her with small highlights. That being one of the great things about being aboard a conjugal chimera. You only retrieve the good parts and embellishment is encouraged without discretion... Maryellen took full ownership of a Cheshire cat grin.

Katie on the other hand slowly coasted through a downhill of Jack being Jack. The mantle of widowhood was as uncomfortable to her as a shoe too small. The more she walked the worse it felt. Jack and she had melded into a conjugation of souls and she felt as if she had been halved like a pear. The night times would not allow her to escape into busy stuff. She had been awake for a long time and there was no shrinkage in her sorrow. In fact, the deficit of his loss grew to where she could not breath. The only word she could think of to describe her station was, Shattered. Her pieces were scattered hither and yon. Her question was, can they be gathered together again? She knew they would never construct as before.

A horn blew in the driveway. Maryellen popped up to look out the window. She said, "They're here to pick us up for the delivery."

The girls quickly threw things in bags to go, made a cup of coffee and walked to the car. All were present. Toliver, who got a good morning kiss. Trip was in the driver's seat beside Cherie, who had one hand on Trip's forearms that doubled as a connection. The limousine was big enough for ten people so everyone was comfortable. Doughnuts had been purchased for all. Trip turned and said, "We have about eight hours, so let me know when a stop is needed." Glances bounced from face to face as they backed out of the driveway.

Renfroe and Ruby, both of whom seemed to have a sexual sheen on their faces were standing in the house doorway with Kalia between them.

Journeys began and ended at the same time.

CPSIA information can be obtained
at www.ICGtesting.com
Printed in the USA
BVHW070856150421
605030BV00010B/1274/J